They had to come up with a story to tell her parents, but he made it so hard to concentrate…

He smoothed her hair away from her face. "You are with me again," he said, smoothing her hair back from her face.

She caressed the golden skin on his chest. "I always want you," she said.

He trailed her hand to her waist, then her hips.

Crap. Tension shot through her. He sat up, sat her on his lap, then stood, wrapping her legs around his waist and carried her to the bathroom. He put her in the bath tub and turned on the water. When the tub was filled, he got in and pulled her against his chest. She felt the familiar tingling and giggled when her tail unfurled. He laughed as he also took sea form, tugging on her necklace to settle it between her breasts.

"We talk now," he said. He held her breasts in his hands. "I always want you," he murmured against her ear.

Focus. She had to focus. "So we tell my parents you're a marine biologist who also studies oceanographic patterns."

Becca Paxton spends her days trying to cover news and write stories for a newspaper on Hawaii's Garden Island to please her bitchy editor. She spends her nights asleep in the arms of a dream lover with sandy brown hair, turquoise eyes, and a toned surfer's body who takes her to sexual heights she never knew existed. Problem is Ethan is a merman who knows Becca's destiny lies with him under the sea, and she's afraid of vast expanses of water. He's wanted her and waited for her since he first glimpsed her in the crystals many earth years ago. Can he convince her she really is a sea form, as he is, and he is really the man of her dreams? And can she leave her life on land and the parents she loves to be with him in a strange world?

KUDOS for *In the Depths*

In Tara Eldana's *In the Depths*, Becca Baxton has left her home on the US mainland and moved to Hawaii's garden island to work for a newspaper and deal with erotic dreams that make her think she's going crazy. What she doesn't know is that the man in her dreams is real, a merman, and waiting for her beneath the waves, a place she is terrified to go. But if he is to claim her, she must overcome her fears and accompany him to his underwater world of her own free will—something she isn't sure she can do. Like the first book in the series, *Under the Riptides*, the story is filled with charming characters, intrigue, and steamy sex scenes. What more do you need on a rainy day with a hot cup of tea? ~ *Taylor Jones, The Review Team of Taylor Jones & Regan Murphy*

In the Depths by Tara Eldana is the second in her mermaid series. In this installment, Becca Paxton is a reporter for a local newspaper on the garden island in Hawaii. By day, she struggles to please her persnickety editor and, by night, she has steamy sex with a dream lover. But dreams are harmless, right? Unfortunately, Becca isn't sure, since her mother suffers from a mental condition and Becca's afraid she might be getting it too—especially when she starts seeing her dream lover in the daytime. Ethan, the dream lover, is really a merman who has left his underwater home to claim his woman. But "sea forms" are only allowed on land for three days, so he doesn't have much time to convince her to leave her entire life behind and travel with him to his home in the depths of the sea. Will the passion they share and the bond that connects them be enough? Ethan doesn't know, particularly when her parents interfere. *In the Depths* is a worthy addition to the series, with charming characters, fast-paced action, and very hot love scenes—a fun, exciting, and arousing escape into the world of "if only" and "I wish." Don't miss it. ~ *Regan Murphy, The Review Team of Taylor Jones & Regan Murphy*

ACKNOWLEDGMENTS

To Lauri Wellington; fabulous Faith; Jack, the art wizard; and everyone at Black Opal Books for giving me a chance to tell my stories.

And the Greater Detroit Romance Writers of America. Without you, this would not be.

And my family, for their patience and understanding with deadlines, edits, and quiet time for writing.

In
the
Depths

Tara Eldana

A Black Opal Books Publication

GENRE: STEAMY ROMANCE/PARANORMAL ROMANCE

This is a work of fiction. Names, places, characters and incidents are either the product of the author's imagination or are used fictitiously, and any resemblance to any actual persons, living or dead, businesses, organizations, events or locales is entirely coincidental. All trademarks, service marks, registered trademarks, and registered service marks are the property of their respective owners and are used herein for identification purposes only. The publisher does not have any control over or assume any responsibility for author or third-party websites or their contents.

DEDICATION

For everyone who has looked at the shimmering ocean

or lake and wondered...what if?

Chapter 1

Damn her editor. She was such a hard ass.

Becca Paxton tried for the fifth time to reach a town councilwoman for a comment following a stupid remark she'd made at the council table during a meeting. Councilwoman Franks was obviously dodging Becca's calls and the copy desk was waiting.

The council meeting had run past midnight after she'd pulled an eight-hour day before the meeting. Becca was at the end of her eight-hour shift—and her patience.

Her focus was shot. She couldn't write another word if she had to.

Sleep—she wanted sleep and the delicious, blue-eyed, sandy-haired man who'd taken over her dreams.

They were so real she felt herself flushing and wet just thinking about him.

"Cheryl," she called to her editor, "she won't answer or call back. I left her my office and cell number."

Cheryl peered at her over her reading glasses. "Did you text her?"

Mike, her colleague, looked over at her, rolled his eyes, and winced.

Becca gritted her teeth. "I don't have her cell phone number. City Hall wouldn't give it to me."

Cheryl stared at her laptop and didn't answer her.

Fuck this.

"I'm heading out," Becca said. She packed her laptop in its soft case and slung it and her purse over her shoulder.

Mike followed her out. They both paused for a beat in the parking lot. Becca felt the island breeze on her skin and watched as the sun slipped closer toward the ocean.

"It's easy to forget this, isn't it?" Mike said.

They were both island transplants from small towns in the Midwest and hired in at the *Kauai Gazette* on the same day.

"Got any plans?" he said.

She and Mike were only friends. He was deliriously happy with Cerissa, who Becca found offbeat, quirky, sweet, and delightful.

"Sleep," she said. "Lots of it. I may actually use my comp time tomorrow."

"Glenn from sports keeps asking me about you. Have lunch with the guy. Put him out of his misery."

Becca laughed. "I'll think about it. Go home to Cerissa."

He waved goodbye, and she stowed her computer in the backseat of her Corolla. She glanced in her rearview mirror and cringed. Haggard blue eyes ringed with dark circles stared back at her. She'd pulled her shoulder-length blonde hair, which had lightened a bit in the island sun, into a pony tail which only drew more attention to her pale skin.

She'd only dated a couple guys since she got the staff writer job a year ago. Eager to get a foothold and make a name for herself, she'd focused on her job and worked a lot of nights on her beat. She should let Mike fix her up with Glenn.

He was hot and real. An island native, his dark hair and eyes and firm, heavy-set build turned more than one female head.

So why did she only want to shut her eyes so a guy with a lean, surfer's body and amazing hands could do things to her she'd never done with anybody when she was awake?

She pulled into her apartment complex as her cell phone pinged.

It was a text from Councilwoman Franks.

Fuck.

She texted Cheryl the councilwoman's response,

copied and pasted it into Cheryl's email, called her editor's desk phone and left a message. She called Councilwoman Franks back, but she didn't answer.

Her text had been delivered. She sent another asking her to confirm receipt and added that she'd called Franks, but got no response.

Cheryl texted back *yes*, no "good job," no "nice follow up," or even "thank-you."

Becca rested her head on her steering wheel. She loved Kauai, known as the Garden Island, even though she was terrified to swim in the vast expanse of the ocean, something she'd only discovered after she moved from the mainland.

She did fine in pools. She'd grown up in Fort Wayne, Indiana, and had made occasional trips with her family up to Lake Michigan when she was growing up. She never went in past her waist and only put her feet into the Pacific.

Her younger brother and sister, Keith and Cara, who were inseparable as children and still close, dove without fear into the whitecaps while she dogpaddled close to shore, the odd one out.

Her father spent most of his time making sure her mother took her anti-psychotic meds. Becca wasn't asked to join in her younger siblings antics, which seemed silly to her, anyway.

So Becca grew up with her nose stuck in a book, magazine, or newspaper and joined Keith and Cara out-

side for a game of horse or burn, only at her parents' urg-
ing.

Someone tapped on the window.

She jumped. Cold sweat trickled down her back.
How could she have left herself so vulnerable? She kept
her hand on her cell phone.

The police she talked to on the crime part of her beat
always said not to fight for property.

She turned her head to look at the person who
knocked.

It was him—the guy from her dreams.

Was she falling prey to her mother's mental illness?

"No," she screamed.

Another car pulled next to her and the guy standing
beside her car was gone.

The older lady in the other vehicle didn't spare her a
glance as she got out of her car, her ear glued to a cell
phone.

Shaking, Becca got out of her car, stood on unsteady
legs, grabbed her stuff, walked into the building, got on
the elevator, and made her way to her third floor apartment. She dropped her stuff on her tiny kitchen table.

She didn't think her dreams could be a sign of psy-
chosis. Her dream man did not ask her to harm herself or
others.

The last thing she wanted now was to shut her eyes.
She sank into her couch and did a search on her cell
phone on symptoms of schizophrenia and bipolar disor-
der.

Was she experiencing a brief psychotic episode? Some of the symptoms fit—seeing and feeling things that weren't there. The information said these episodes were triggered by severe stress, such as death of a loved one or a natural disaster. A cranky editor didn't qualify.

Her heart, which had been hammering in her chest since the knock on her car window, slowed and against her will her eyes closed, pulling her into a dreamless sleep.

❧❧❧

Ethan paced the great hall of the Garnet City. What was he thinking startling Becca like that when she was so mentally exhausted? His sire Thobian said he was impatient and told him to wait, but his need to touch her in her waking state was too strong.

It was easy to slip through the portal and bridge time and space because the autumnal equinox drew near. He'd looked into the quartz crystals a full earth year ago and saw Becca, his twin flame. His life and world had come alive and made sense.

She didn't know her destiny was with him under the vast expanse of ocean that she feared. He had taken her in her dreams, repeatedly, to their mutual delight.

Lovion, the ranking member of the Ruling Council, smirked. "She screamed at the sight of you. She must come with you *willingly*."

"Her mother's illness makes her fearful," Thobian said. Ethan's sire held a seat on the Ruling Council but cast only one vote. In cases of deadlock, Lovion cast the deciding vote, and he hated land dwellers, even those who could take sea form.

"She is mine," Ethan said it quietly and calmly. The members of the council, except for Thobian, looked shocked at Ethan's words. Lovion sneered.

"He can be spared from his duties for a time," Thobian said.

Sea forms ensured to their best ability that under water ecosystems remained viable in the wake of natural disruptions and those caused by land forms.

Ethan's mother Lara and his sire Thobian chanted ancient words of protection. Ethan bowed his head in thanks. He grabbed a triangular quartz crystal and the ruby necklace he would give to Becca to signify their joining, sheathed his lucky knife, and headed through the winding caverns to the portal.

ℰᔆℰᔆ

Becca sat on the beach and watched the surfers. She tried not to think about work. Things were heating up in the local election coming up in November in the town she covered as part of her beat. She loved writing about crime, education, and human interest stories, but she didn't like the government part of her beat. She checked the time. She had agreed to have lunch with Glenn from sports. He covered high school sports and worked lots of nights, so lunch worked out best.

Becca glanced at the surfers. One caught her attention. He had golden skin over a lean, toned swimmer's body and sun streaked hair like the guy in her hallucination. How many surfers looked like that in Kauai?

She gathered her things as the surfer drew closer. She needed to get ready for her lunch date.

She sat inside at Zeke's restaurant, a Kauai institution, waiting for Glenn. He'd texted to say an editorial meeting had run late and he was on his way. She looked at the mermaid carved of wood that hung near the bar.

An exquisite necklace had been carved so it hung just above her bare breasts. Her tail was resplendent in shades of crimson and turquoise.

"It's a persistent legend." It was Glenn. He kissed her cheek and took a seat across from her. "Sorry, my editor—"

Becca laughed. "Say no more."

They placed their orders, shrimp for her and Mahi Mahi for him. Her eyes were drawn back to the carving.

Glenn smiled and squeezed her hand. Disappointingly, she felt no spark. He felt warm and comforting, like a friend. "The old-timers say their elders believed they existed."

Her thoughts strayed to her dream lover and the surfer. "Do you surf?" she said.

He kept hold of her hand. "Sure." He chuckled. "I grew up here, so yeah. Went to U-H then came right back to this rock. Borin' huh? Why did you come?"

"I don't think it's boring," she said. "I don't know why I came here. I needed a job, but there are newspapers and TV stations in Fort Wayne, where I grew up."

"A Hoosier."

"Yep," she said, making her voice sound as flat and Midwestern as she could.

He laughed, still holding her hand. "You're beautiful. You could be on camera."

She shuddered. "I barely passed my speech class at I-U. If you put a mic in my face, I can't string two words together."

"I'm glad you're here," he said, letting go of her hand when his cell phone vibrated.

"My editor," he said. "One second." He ended the call quickly and they finished their food. The shrimp was succulent and beyond delicious.

She stared at the carving of the mermaid. "The detail is unbelievable," she said, popping the last bite of shrimp into her mouth.

"There are males, too," Glenn said, "allegedly."

She laughed at his reporter-speak.

"Do you miss your family?" he asked.

Did she? "I was never especially close to my brother and sister. They're still in college, I-U and Purdue. My parents—my mother's fine when she's on her meds." She dropped her gaze. "She doesn't always take them, she feels good, and then she stops. And Dad has to keep a sharp eye on her. He's a cop, so he doesn't miss much."

"That's rough," he said.

"Not always. She's great when she's great," she said.

He reached for her hand as his phone vibrated again. "Deadlines," he muttered. He put cash on the table. "I got to get back. Stay and have dessert if you want." He kissed her cheek and squeezed her shoulder. "Are you busy Friday night?"

Before she could answer, he said, "I'll call you, 'kay?"

She smiled and he left her. She admired the way he moved through the room with an athlete's grace for such a big, solid guy, but she felt—nothing, not one tingle.

She didn't want dessert so the waiter brought her a selection of tea bags.

❧❦❧

Ethan wanted to physically remove the island dweller's hands from Becca's skin. He forced himself to take deep, even breaths until the dark-haired land dweller put his mouth on her cheek and hand on her shoulder. Ethan stood so fast the chair he sat on fell to the ground behind him, startling some elders sitting near him.

He smiled in apology, righted the chair, and made his way to Becca.

Chapter 2

She picked out some oolong tea and dropped it into her cup.

"Becca?"

It was him—dream/hallucination guy. He wore a black T-shirt, cargo shorts and flip flops. His shoulder-length streaky blond hair was tied back off his face revealing a square jawline and smooth-shaven face.

She watched in horror as he sat across from her. She rubbed her temples and shut her eyes. This couldn't be happening.

"Anything for you, sir?" the waiter said.

She gasped. The waiter could see him?

"I think there is water, enough," he said, taking the cup Glenn had not used. The waiter left them.

"He can see you," she whispered.

"We must speak," he said.

She struggled to breathe.

He grasped her hand, the same one Glenn had. A jolt of heat shot straight to her core. She stared at him.

"May we leave this place?"

The waiter returned. He looked concerned. "Are you okay?" He looked only at her, not sparing dream guy a glance. "Are you afraid of him? We can call the police."

Was she scared of the man holding her hand as if he would never let it go? She felt her hand curl into his. No, she wasn't scared of him. This felt strangely right.

She smiled at the waiter. "No, I was just surprised to see him is all. Thank you for asking."

"Okay," the waiter said, taking away the dirty plates.

"We may leave?" He said it like a question, keeping firm hold of her hand.

There were benches overlooking the water a bit past the parking lot. She wanted to stay in a public place. "Yes." She pointed to the benches and they walked hand-in-hand.

"I am Ethan," he said.

"How do you know my name?"

They reached the bench, and he drew her down next to him so they were touching.

"You are not ill." He touched her cheek. "You do not share mother's sickness," he said.

She pulled her hand out of his grasp and stood up. This was beyond weird. "Who are you, and how do you know this stuff?"

He stood, too. "Your dreams, our dreams, are real." He held out his hand. "We go to water. I show you."

She locked her purse in the trunk of her car and he led her to the water's edge. Amazingly, there was nobody on the beach.

"No surf here," he said, as if he could read her thoughts. He ran his eyes over her bare legs and short skirt. "We sit in sand so I show you."

He crouched down, uncaring if the waves soaked his shorts. He patted a spot in the wet sand between his legs. "Here, Becca." He said her name melodically.

"My skirt," she said.

"You could keep it on if you slip off your underthings," he said.

She looked around. The beach was deserted. What the hell?

"Okay," she said. She stood, slipped off her sandals and pulled down her panties, keeping her skirt in place. Feeling daring, she pulled her shirt off, leaving her lacy bra on. He kicked off his flip flops, took off his shirt, pulled something out of his cargo shorts then pulled those off, too. He wore only a loin cloth. He hid their clothes and flip-flops under some huge rocks and came back to her.

His eyes blazed silver. Smiling, he held his hand out.

She took it and felt the spark again. He chuckled, tugged her down onto the sand, and settled her between his thighs. He moved her hair aside, pressed a kiss to her nape, and fastened a long, heavy necklace of huge red stones around her throat.

Its weight felt oddly right. She fingered the stones that glittered like red flames in the Hawaiian sun. "It's like the mermaid carving in the restaurant," she said.

A wave pounded into the sand up to her waist. The skirt billowed in the water and her legs felt sticky and tingly from the salt water.

Tingly?

He pinched her hip when another wave crested, dragging then a bit farther into the ocean. Her chest felt tight with fear, although her butt still touched the bottom. When the wave ebbed she glanced down.

Her legs were gone.

She had a tail, a beautiful crimson and gold tail. It felt so right. Amazingly, her fear dissolved as she wiggled her tail and squealed in joy. If this was a dream, she didn't want to wake up.

He slipped his hands under her bra and tweaked her nipples until she groaned. "You like sea form?" Ethan said against her ear. "We are the same—" He said a word she didn't understand.

Was it an endearment? He took hold of her chin. "The dreams when we join are real," he said. "My home is Garnet City." He ran his tongue over his straight white teeth. "Would you like to see it?"

She clutched his rock hard thigh. "But you aren't—your legs."

"Because I do not wish it just yet."

How could this be real? None of it made logical sense. What if this was all a hallucination?

He pressed his mouth to hers for the briefest moment. "You are not ill, Becca. This is real. I am from under the sea. There is a sea form we believe makes her home here with a land form. We have not confirmed this."

Cerissa, Mike's girlfriend, immediately came to her mind. He was so protective of her and she used odd turns of phrase like Ethan did.

Becca stared into his eyes, feeling like she could drown in the turquoise depths. "It's like you are reading my thoughts," she said.

She traced his firm mouth with her fingers. His words came to her, although he didn't move his lips. "Sea forms must do this under the waves. Twin flames, joined sea forms, may also do this when they wish. We have joined partly in our dreams."

"I heard you but you didn't speak," she whispered.

He kissed her fingers. "You come to Garnet City?" He had taken sea form in magnificent shades of midnight blue and sunset orange.

She looked out over the vast sea and panicked. Her chest hurt. "Ethan, I don't swim in the ocean." Her throat was closing up and she struggled to breathe. "All this water. I'm so sorry. I can't."

He caressed her cheek. "Look at me, Becca. I keep you close, always. There is portal. We don't swim far."

She wanted to go and make him happy. She had never cared this much about any guy before. If she didn't count the sex dreams, she still had her V-card.

But why did he want her? How was this happening? She was just a girl from Indiana who got on a plane to work for a tiny newspaper on a rocky island.

"I see you in crystals," he said. "You are untouched." He phrased it like a fact, rather than a question.

"But our dreams?" she said. She'd given herself to him without restraint repeatedly. But she'd felt no pain. Didn't it pinch the first time?

His lips quirked into a smile. "Is different in waking state. Is better."

Her cheeks flamed. She'd lost count of the times she'd awoken in the throes of powerful orgasm—nothing like her college roommates talked about—but alone.

"We are destined," he said. "Will you come to my home?"

She forgot about the endless expanse of ocean that she was nothing in. She forgot about the story on the zoning ordinance she hadn't started. She let herself get lost in his smile and the feel of her glorious tail. She smiled. "Yes."

He took hold of her waist and kissed her. His tongue plunged in and out of her mouth the same way he slid inside her in her dreams.

"No dream, Becca." His mouth fused to hers and plunged them under water. She struggled and he pulled his mouth away. She gasped then calmed, realizing she could breathe under water.

But everything was murky. She was swimming blind. He had tight hold of her waist and propelled them powerfully through the water to an underground cave infused with light. He kissed her and she was lost to everything except his touch.

He released her and lifted her shoulders out of the water. Her breasts were bare. He had removed her bra at some point in the journey.

"We are home," he said.

Pink crystal formations stood stark against a pink sky. He helped her out of the water and pulled her against him. She shivered with nerves.

"You are not ill as your mother," he said.

"How do you know about my mother?" she snapped, pulling away from him. Always she felt protective of her mother. Janet suffered from schizophrenia and was also bipolar. She was sweet and funny and kind—when she stayed on her meds.

"I see you suffer when she is ill," he said.

Her tail tingled and her legs, now completely hairless, took shape. Her sex felt different against the sodden skirt and she looked under it. She was smooth everywhere. Only the hair on her arms and head remained.

She looked at his honed, hairless chest.

"You are sea form now," he said.

She forgot he could read her thoughts. He stood, clad only in a loincloth. A sheath also hung loosely around his rock hard abs. Did all the males here look like him?

He pulled her gently to her feet, scowled, and tugged on her necklace. "In Garnet City this means I claim you, Becca. You belong to me, only me." Pulling her close, he lifted her into his arms and wrapped her legs around his waist as if she weighed nothing. Was he jealous?

He kissed her as if he was starved for her. His erection pressed the apex of her thighs, more sensitive now that she was smooth. She rubbed her sex against him. When he lifted his mouth, he was breathing hard.

She caressed his face. "There's only you. I haven't been with anyone but you, on land or sea." She giggled at the trite "land or sea" phrase.

He raised his eyebrows, looking puzzled. "Land or sea is cliché, overused."

"Never mind," she said. "I was curious about this place, is all."

He slid her down his body. "I need to sink inside you but we must say words in joining in great hall, first, I think."

He threaded his fingers through hers as they walked toward the glittering red pillars. She stopped each time they passed a waterfall or burst of floral blooms that re-minded her of hibiscus.

Her mother loved flowers and dolphins. They walked

along deep channels to what she assumed was the entrance to the city proper. He stopped her.

"Look," he said. A dolphin swam alongside them in the channel and lifted its head out of the water.

She laughed. "You read my thoughts."

"So did she, it seems," he said. "She welcomes you."

Becca crouched down to touch the smiling mammal. "She?"

"I will teach you how to see if dolphin is he or she."

The dolphin made a noise. "She'll give you a ride if you want," he said.

She'd never swam with a dolphin. It was on her bucket list of things to do in Hawaii, but she hadn't gotten to it.

"Come," he said. He eased her into the water and pinched her waist until her tail unfurled. She squealed in joy. He chuckled and the dolphin made a high-pitched wail.

Ethan chanted words in his language. His voice was as good, or better than the finalists on "American Idol" or "The Voice."

"It's beautiful," she said. His eyes traveled from her face to her breasts, to her russet and powder blue tail. "Yes," he said.

"I love my...how you say?...sea form. But, your voice. It's awesome."

He palmed her breasts. "What is awesome?"

"Good, but better, best," she said.

He kissed her until the dolphin nudged them apart.

"She is jealous, like I am when island dweller touch your skin and you smile at him," he said, scowling.

She kissed him, trying to show him with her mouth what she couldn't put into words, yet. She was cautious by nature. The guys in college said she was a cold bitch, some thought she was gay because she had no real interest in any of them.

She knew now she had been waiting for Ethan. The dolphin nudged them apart again.

Becca petted her long nose. "I'm going to name you Nudge," she said.

Ethan showed her how to hold onto Nudge's fins so she could swim on the dolphin's back. "I will be near," he said.

👁️‍🗨️

"You wish this?"

Her answer meant so much to him. She looked toward the Garnet City and at him. Her eyes went soft—gray-blue like the sea above the waves under a sky filled with clouds.

"Yes, I wish this," she said.

He longed to kiss her but the dolphin lurched forward, impatient to be on their way.

"Holy hell," she said.

Nudge plunged the water for brief spurts so Becca's

head was mostly above the water, as if the dolphin knew Becca was a new sea form, yet to learn her fins.

"Ethan?" she cried out in alarm as she lost her grip on the dolphin's fins.

He took hold of her and lifted her, them, out of the channel, hauling her into his arms so he could kiss her. How had he done without her?

The more he tasted her lips, her skin, and felt her go boneless in his arms, the more he wanted her. He could not wait until after the ceremony. He had waited long enough.

He pulled himself free of his loincloth and plunged his finger into her sex. She was so wet for him, he nearly spilled his seed. He set her on his lap so she straddled him and lowered her onto his rigid cock as slowly as he could.

When he came to her barrier, he looked into her beautiful eyes in question.

"Yes," she whispered.

He pressed his thumb to her sensitive pearl and thrust into her, breaching her barrier. She took long, deep breaths. She was tight and he restrained himself from thrusting deeper because he did not wish to cause her further pain.

"It's good, I'm okay," she said, lowering herself deeper onto his cock.

He groaned. "Becca, I must go slow."

"No, darling." She caressed his sac and he was lost.

He plunged into her silken sheath, lifting her up and down, pumping into her until she rained on his cock, shimmering in his arms. He emptied himself inside her and held her, finally forcing himself to lift her and settle her between his legs.

She glanced down and gasped when she saw her virgin's blood on their bodies.

"We can't go into the city like this," she said, biting her lip.

He moved her hair aside so he could kiss her nape. "I care not," he said.

She looked around at the deserted pathway along the channel. "What if someone had seen us?"

He shrugged. "All wait in the great hall."

She'd called him darling. He knew that to be an endearment. He loved that word on her lips. It warmed his blood. But did she feel shame in their joining because she believed all would see the evidence of it?

She tugged her skirt down. His mother said female land dwellers exercised modesty and explained how it was different in different places on land.

"You are modest and not with shame for joining with me?"

"Yes—no," she said. "Yes to the first part and no I am not ashamed. But will those in your city will think I am easy—that I would join with many males since we joined here where anyone could see?"

"No one saw us, darling," he said, watching her

smile when he said darling. "But it will be known we have joined and you are only mine. I will later explain."

Grasping her around her waist, he lowered her legs into the channel then pulled her up. He splashed water onto his legs, removing evidence of their first joining in their bodies, except for the spot on his loincloth. He'd keep that scrap of cloth until he ceased to be.

She shivered.

"The skirt makes you cold." Over her protests, he removed it. "We will be given garments before we speak words in great hall."

"Okay," she said, yawning. He picked her up and carried her the rest of the way into the city while she laid head against his shoulder and drifted into slumber.

For the first time since he learned his fins, he felt at peace.

Chapter 3

She opened her eyes in a room filled with crystals in every shape and every shade in the rainbow. Flat on her back, naked, on a raised platform surrounded by males and females with long white hair wearing blue robes, she didn't see Ethan.

She tried to sit up. She felt hands on her shoulders, Ethan's hands. "I am here."

She turned to look at him. He wore a purple robe. His blond streaky hair was tied back from his face. He stole her breath away. He looked like a movie star. She caressed his jaw and he pressed a kiss into her palm.

Those around them smiled.

"What is happening?" she asked.

"Healers ensuring you are unharmed," he said, smiling. "You are perfect." He slipped a purple robe that matched his over her head, tugging her necklace over the silky fabric. "You must prepare for great hall."

He helped her down from the platform and led her to a chamber, then left her. She sat on a cushioned bench while two young females swept her hair into an elaborate updo threaded with tiny sparkling crystals. Then they rubbed oil that smelled like lilacs onto her arms, legs and feet and gently patted it on her face.

Was this the sea form equivalent of a wedding ceremony?

They smoothed a pink tint on her lips and cheeks, murmuring words she didn't understand. Were they talking about her? Were they angry she was there?

As if they sensed her anxiety, they smiled—genuine, sweet smiles—and she let out the breath she didn't realize she'd been holding.

"Our English bad," the smaller sea form said. "French better."

Becca smiled. "My French sucks."

Both sea forms made sucking noises and they all erupted in peals of laughter. The taller sea form touched the ruby necklace. "Ethan learn English when he see you in crystal. He no join with female in Garnet City after that."

Another female in a turquoise robe with eyes the

same color as Ethan's and streaky blonde hair that hung in a thick braid over one shoulder entered the chamber and the young sea forms smiled and left.

The older female carried a flower that looked like hibiscus and held it out to her.

Becca closed her hand around the stem and smiled. Was this her bridal bouquet?

"Ethan my son. I am Lara. Ethan so happy. He wait so long for you. Is time."

Fighting nerves, Becca followed Lara through a series of chambers on a floor that felt like marble and walls that looked like opaque rose quartz. Lara's feet were also bare and looked somewhat web like. Glancing down at her own feet, Becca noticed they seemed wider than before.

They entered what she assumed was the great hall. Lara touched her shoulder and looked at a male standing on the platform with a dozen other sea forms. "Is Lovion. He opposes joining. Ethan's sire Thobian and I watch him, protect you."

Protect her?

Lara lowered her head and chanted words in the language of the sea forms. The crowd, at least one hundred by Becca's guess, joined in the chant.

Elaborate chandelier-like formations hung from the cathedral ceiling, somehow reflecting light into the space. The crowd wore robes in shades of white, blue, and green. Only she and Ethan wore purple. Lara urged her forward to where Ethan waited. Lovion glared at her with such hatred as she approached, she shuddered and her steps faltered.

Ethan made a move toward her but something Lovion said stopped him. Lara was at her side. "Free will," she whispered. "You must do this with free will."

Ethan looked angry.

He insisted she did not share her mother's illness. But what was this? What was happening to her?

Feeling faint, she swallowed hard as the room went black.

ာ၁ာ

"Becca?" Ethan said her name in the musical way she loved so much. She opened her eyes, and felt his breath against her cheek. She was settled between his legs on a bed in a chamber she hadn't seen before.

She tried to swivel and look at him but he pressed his cheek to hers, selfie-style, and held a bite of shrimp to her lips. "Eat, darling. I wish so much to join with you, I forget you must take food."

On cue, her stomach rumbled. He chuckled as she chewed the succulent shrimp. He pressed a small crystal goblet filled with amber liquid that smelled like peaches to her lips and she guzzled it down. It was light, sweet with a bit of tart, and fruity.

Ethan sighed. "I rush you and not take care for you. We join in great hall when you feel strong."

He continued to feed her bites of shrimp and something white and crunchy that reminded her of water chestnuts. "You are well?" he said.

"Yes."

Was she? He kissed her nape and moved her to the edge of the bed. He stood first. His turquoise eyes raked over her. She stared at his movie-star jawline and firm, full lips. Her mouth dried and heat flooded her core. How could he, or this, be real?

She was a bookworm from Fort Wayne covering City Council meetings for a tough editor on a tiny island in paradise.

That part was magical. She'd applied on a whim and beaten out dozens for the job.

He held out his hand. She took it and picked up the hibiscus. They walked a different route to the great hall than the one she and Lara had taken, this time along channels and narrow, winding corridors.

He swept her into his arms and kissed her. His erection pressed against her and she rubbed her body on his.

He lifted his mouth from hers and groaned. "Always around you, I am like this," he murmured. "For no other female, I am this way."

"It is the same for me," she said.

He took her mouth again when a loud squeal erupted from the channel. She instinctively sought protection in his arms. He grunted as if it pleased him then laughed. "It is your dolphin. She is telling you, how you say, best wishes."

Nudge squealed, then smiled.

"She is your fan."

Fan, he said fan?

He frowned. "Is that right word?"

She traced his beautiful mouth with her fingertips. "Your English is wonderful. And your voice, I could listen to it forever. But I must learn your language and your ways," she said.

"We have forever, darling. Come, they wait."

The great hall was as it was before. Had the sea forms waited all this time? How long had it been since she first arrived here?

"I'm sorry for making you wait," she said as loud as she could, clutching her bloom.

A collective gasp went through the crowd. Lovion roared from the platform. Ethan stepped away from her and walked stiffly to the platform. Was he angry with her?

Lara moved from where she had been standing near the platform through the crowd to her side. "You say 'sorry.' Sea forms know this word. They think you sorry to be in Garnet City, not wish to join with Ethan."

"No," Becca said loudly. "I made everyone wait. That is what I meant."

Lara held her hand up, as if to silence her. "You must show joy to join with my son, that you do so with free will."

The crowd cleared as she made her way to Ethan.

Facing him, unsure of what do to, she sank to her knees and just let the words come from her heart. "I choose this. I wish to join with you. I—"

A woman with white hair who stood next to Lovion held up her hand, as Lara had done, then nodded to the crowd, bowed her head, and chanted in a clear, soprano tones worthy of the opera stage. The sea forms around her joined in. Ethan held out his hand to Becca and pulled her to her feet.

Lovion ignored them. She turned to Ethan. She had so much to learn about the Garnet City. She squared her shoulders. That was what she did…wasn't it?…go into new situations, figure out what was happening, pick out the threads of a story, and write it in such a way that people could understand. She could make sense of this.

The chanting stopped. Ethan smiled. "Forever, it is done," he said.

Was she supposed to repeat those words, like wedding vows?

"Forever, it is done," she said.

Applause erupted. Ethan released her hand. She glanced at Lovion, still blatantly ignoring them. She raised her middle finger at him, although he likely didn't see it and probably had no idea what it meant.

Ethan lifted her into his arms and carried her to a chamber filled with food. Hundreds of crystals set in various spots reflected light. The final part of the joining ceremony took place there. Her cheeks flamed.

⟳⟳⟳

He sealed the chamber and shrugged out of his robe. A feast awaited them. Shells piled high with the bounty of the sea were arranged on a sideboard. He would never overlook her need to take sustenance again and would see to her every need for the rest of his existence.

Joy, such as he had never known, swamped him like the waves the land forms who surfed so coveted. She stared at the food, then at him. Her hand strayed to her hair.

Was she shy of him?

He took her in his arms, eased her out of her robe, and took hold of her chin. Her eyes held the gray color of the sea during a storm. Was she afraid? Did she regret joining with him?

He said her name in the musical lilt that seemed to soothe her. She went soft in his arms and pressed her cheek to where his heart thundered in his chest.

"What happens now? I don't know what to do," she said.

He chuckled and eased them down to the bed. "My scribe wonders what comes next in the story."

He palmed her breasts, teasing her nipples into stiff points begging for his mouth. "This—us," he said pressing kisses to her nape.

She sighed and he was lost. Wrapping her legs around his hips, he plunged into her slick, wet channel.

Her tightness felt like softest silk. She was always wet for him. Would he ever get enough of her, of this?

He pumped into her, hitting the back of her womb and the spot she loved until she clenched around him, raining her sweet honey on his cock, and screamed his name. Only then did he empty himself inside her.

Spent, he collapsed on top of her, then moved so they were side by side, but he was still inside her.

"Always I am impatient," he said. "I rush you."

She covered his mouth with her soft hand. "That was amazing. I thought this, the way you make me feel only happened in books. I didn't think it was real. I'm still not sure it is. My mother has bad spells when she thinks things are happening that aren't."

He pressed a kiss into her palm and slowly pulled out of her and went to the sideboard. He set a shell of food next to the bed then filled a goblet with the liquid she enjoyed before. "Take food and drink. You mostly doubt when you need these things."

She sat up and looked at him in surprise. "I do?"

He gave her the goblet and she drank it all. He smiled. "I think, yes."

He settled her between his legs and fed her bites of lobster and seaweed until she waved him off. "I'm stuffed."

He turned her so she was on her lap and he could look at her. "Is stuffed bad?"

She had color in her cheeks and her eyes shone like the skies above the sea on a stormy day.

"No, I am not hungry, not for food." She stroked his erection. He dispensed with the food and circled her nipples with his finger.

"I love you, Ethan. I know this is beyond fast, but I do."

His heart soared.

"I see you in the crystals," he said, moving his hand lower to her smooth mound. She sighed. "I love you from then," he said. "Others laugh."

She arched into his hand, and he pressed down on her clit. She came, moaning his name.

"We are fully joined," he said. "You are as me. I make you so."

She trailed kisses down his chest to his waist, then lower, sucking on the tip of his cock. She looked up at him through her lashes. "I want to please you."

She took him in her mouth and he slid in and out of her beautiful lips before he pulled her away from him to fuse his mouth to his and piston into her. He pressed her sex as he spilled his seed. It dripped down her leg. He burned the sight into his brain.

He thought of her belly round with their child. She wanted his baby, didn't she? They'd never spoken of it.

He took hold of her chin. Her eyes were wide. "Becca—"

"I heard your thoughts," she said. She smiled. "Yes, I

want your babies. I never did before. You're my game changer." She frowned. "But how does that work now that I'm like you. I don't know anything about your home. And why does Lovion hate me?"

Ethan picked up a quartz crystal, settled her in his arms, and set the crystal on her forehead. It would transmit scenes of life in the Garnet City. "Our home, darling."

He would explain about Lovion's nonsense later.

She giggled. "The children must learn to swim."

"Is fin class," he said, loving the way she fit perfectly against him. "You must also learn your fins. Is same as babies learning to use legs."

"Will you teach me?" she said.

"Yes," he breathed into her ear.

She closed her eyes and touched the crystal. "It's like a foreign movie when the voices don't match the pictures. But the sound is in my mind, like your thoughts are sometimes."

She went stiff against him and gasped. "Now I'm seeing the newsroom where I work. Ethan, my mother is there, alone. My father's not with her. Is this really happening? She looks upset. This is not good."

Cursing, he donned his robe and held hers out to her. "We look in other crystals."

She slipped the robe over her head. He sheathed his knife then took her hand and led her out of the chamber. Her hair was mostly swept off her neck although some strands hung against the beautiful lines of her throat.

Fighting a sick sense of dread they would have to leave the Garnet City, he kissed her nape as they made their way to the hall of crystal. Thobian and Lara were there. His sire put his hand on Ethan's shoulder. "She has electronic messages from the other scribe about her mother," Thobian said in the language of the sea forms.

Lara squeezed Becca's hand. "Your mother, she is alone and your sire worries for her. For the next three rotations of the earth, you may bridge time and space through the portal." Lara looked from Becca to him. "You are fully joined?"

Ethan nodded. Sea forms had one chance every four of the earth's months to enter the portal—if they weren't needed on eco missions under the sea—go on land for three earth rotations, and return to the Garnet City. Ethan had spent his chance to bring Becca to the Garnet City.

She was fully joined with him and had shifted to sea form. So she had the same chance to return to land then come back to the Garnet City. If they were together, touching one another as they entered the portal, they could make the journey back to the Garnet City together.

As a new sea form she could adapt to living on land if she decided not to return. However Ethan, as a mature sea form, had to come back to his life under the sea for the pure essence of water that sustained his life form. He could live on land for three earth rotations at a time. If Becca stayed, he would face peril swimming through the deep to return as he would be unable to go through the portal without her.

There were reports that a female sea form lived on the island group that Becca had lived on, and it was not known how she did this without the infusion of the pure essence of water.

Becca trembled. "I have to go." She turned to Lara and Thobian. "You have been so kind and welcoming."

"We will soon see you," Thobian said. "The portal is clear for your journey."

Ethan took off his robe, ensuring his knife was in place around his waist and stood in his loin cloth. He tugged on Becca's robe but Lara stopped him.

"Wait until you reach the portal," she said.

Ethan linked his fingers through Becca's and they followed Lara and Thobian through ancient caverns along the channel. Becca's dolphin swam noisily alongside them, popping her head out of the water to screech at them.

His mother laughed. "She is angry you leave."

Lovion waited at the entrance to the portal, his face twisted into his usual sneer. "Free will," he said. "She must return—"

Thobian cut him off, speaking harshly in the language of the Garnet City, telling the old windbag to leave his family alone and threatening his position on the ruling council, and his being, if he did not do so.

The color had drained from Becca's beautiful face. "What are they saying?"

"Is of no matter," Lara said.

She pressed her hands to Becca and Ethan's shoulders, lowered her head, and chanted words of protection. Thobian joined in as Lovion sidled away. Thobian and Lara left them and Ethan lifted Becca's robe from her trembling body.

He took firm hold of her waist and crushed her to him. His cock was hard as granite against her softness. He fused his mouth to hers, and she went soft and still in his arms. With a force of will he didn't know he possessed, he set her away from him and led her through the portal.

Chapter 4

Becca's legs tingled and she felt her tail unfurl. They clung to a reef and Ethan kissed her, keeping hold of her waist as they submerged and swam through the deep because she couldn't see in the dark water.

They made it to the beach on Kauai, to the same spot they had left from, just as the sun was setting. They sat in the shallows as their land forms took shape.

A female approached them and Becca covered her nudity.

"Becca?" It was Cerissa and she was alone, which was odd because Mike rarely left her side. "Michael waits," she said.

Then she said words Becca didn't understand. Ethan nodded. Cerissa handed her a bag with shorts, T-shirts, and flip flops for both of them. As they dressed, Ethan explained that Cerissa was a sea form who somehow lived on land.

Cerissa watched them and smiled. "You are joined."

He drew Becca against him and pulled her ruby necklace free of the T-shirt.

Cerissa giggled. "Your seed, it grows so soon."

Seed? Did she mean pregnant, already? Holy hell. Becca's hand strayed to her flat belly.

Ethan stood stiff. Was he upset? Did he not want her to be pregnant so soon?

"How do you know, Cerissa?" Becca said.

"Is way of sea forms."

Becca calculated her cycle. The timing was right, although she didn't feel any different. "I want the baby, Ethan. It just happened so fast. All of this has."

"We must go to your mother," he said.

"Michael said she waits in newsroom for you." Ethan miraculously retrieved their clothes and her car keys from where he'd hidden them under boulders.

Her car—how long had they been gone? Would it still be in the restaurant parking lot?

"Cerissa, how did you get here?" she asked.

Cerissa said that Mike had dropped her off. "I text him if you come." They walked to her car. The driver's window had been smashed out and the driver's seat was damp from the rain the fell on the island every day.

Luckily nothing else was damaged and she'd locked her purse in the trunk. It wasn't far to the office. Mike joined them as they walked into the building.

Her mother sat at Becca's desk, sipping coffee from Becca's mug. Glenn sat next to her. It was just past eight. Cheryl was at her desk, which was odd, because she normally left at five o'clock.

Mike said her mother had been there since early afternoon. "She was agitated you weren't here. Cheryl and Glenn explained you took some time off."

Cheryl?

Her mother hadn't seen her yet. "She came alone?" Becca said.

"Yeah," Mike said.

Cerissa came to Mike's side and he pulled her against him. Becca and Ethan stayed out of her mother's view. Becca pulled her cell phone out of her purse and called her dad. He answered on the first ring.

"Becs?"

"Mom's here. On Kauai. At my office."

"She left me a note. I came as soon as I could, but I'm stuck in San Francisco. Flights are delayed."

"I'll sort her out. Call you later. Love you."

She stepped forward. Ethan held on to her shoulder. "Mom?"

"Rebecca?"

Ethan released her as her mother bounced toward her

and Becca bent down from her five-foot-eight inch height to hug her five-foot-two-inch mother. "These handsome guys kept me company," her mother whispered in her ear. "Mike has a girlfriend but the Hawaiian guy is hot. He said you went out."

Becca looked at Ethan. Sea forms, she was learning, had acute hearing. He stepped next to Becca and put his hand on her shoulder, glaring at Glenn.

"Mom, this is Ethan, my—" She faltered. Boyfriend didn't seem right.

"They elope," Cerissa chirped.

"Huh?" Glenn said.

Ethan glared at him.

"Husband?" her mother said.

Cheryl's mouth gaped open.

Ethan took her mother's hand. "I see where Becca finds her beauty."

"I'm Janet," her mother said, awkwardly hugging Ethan.

Glenn kissed Becca's cheek. "Congratulations."

"I'm sorry," Becca said. "It happened so fast."

Glenn squeezed her ring-less left hand. "I guess. No ring yet. See ya."

Ethan bristled beside her.

"I feel so tired all of a sudden," Janet said.

"You need a couple more days off, right?" Cheryl said, frowning.

Had she only been gone for two days? It seemed like a lifetime.

"Yes," Becca said.

"It will be unpaid," Cheryl said. "You don't have any vacation time left."

"I know," Becca said, waiting for her to say congratulations, or acknowledge Ethan.

Nothing.

"Thanks."

Cheryl had already turned her attention to her computer screen.

"Let's go, Mom," Becca said.

"I booked a hotel and took a cab here," her mother said as they made their way out of the building.

"A cab?" Becca said.

Her mother stumbled. Ethan gently took her arm and put her in the back seat of Becca's Corolla.

"Your window." Janet slurred her words. After a manic episode, her mother's energy sank and she would sleep for a day straight.

"Which hotel, Mom?"

She named one close by. They got her up to her room, Janet crawled under the covers fully clothed, and dropped off to sleep. Becca phoned her father, but he didn't pick up. She left a voice mail message with the name of the hotel and room number and asked him to call her so she could pick him up from the airport when he arrived.

She sent a follow up text, and they quietly shut the door.

Then she faced one very pissed off male. She tugged on his hand. "Come on. Let's go back to my place."

They walked silently to her car. His face was a blank mask. They didn't speak until they were in her apartment. She trailed her fingers up his bicep. "You seem upset," she said.

"You let that scribe touch you. Then you say you are sorry we join."

She gripped his broad shoulders. "Land forms touch to congratulate each other. Like sea forms do to chant," she said.

Was she getting through to him? He seemed so distant. She hated it.

She let go of his shoulders to slip her hands under his shirt. He gripped her waist.

Thank fuck.

She looked into his eyes. "I only feel friendship with him, not like when I touch you. Or you touch me. Glenn wanted to go out with me before I saw you on land, but I said no. It was just that one time. And I didn't feel anything. Nothing like this."

She pressed her mouth to his, and he deepened the kiss, pressing his erection against her.

He lifted his mouth and held her tight in his arms. "What is go out?"

"Share a meal," she said. His eyes blazed silver. He

was still angry. "Not like we do. He didn't feed me." She thought of the way she would suck on his fingers. Her face felt hot.

"I saw," he said.

"You did?"

He took hold of her chin and narrowed his eyes. They looked like silver shards. "You not feel anger if different female touch me?"

She wrenched out of his arms. Did sea forms join with more than one female at the same time? She knew nothing of life in the Garnet City.

Bile rose in her throat. She ran to her bathroom and threw up. He was at her side instantly, holding her hair back until her nausea subsided. She rinsed her mouth with toothpaste before she faced Ethan.

His smile was tender. "No, darling. You are only one I join with. And you will have no other."

"You read my thoughts. I keep forgetting."

He lifted her in his arms as if she weighed nothing and set her down on the bed. "You take food."

She had nothing in her fridge. "I'll order pizza," she said. She had the strongest craving for anchovies. She took her cell phone out of the pocket of her shorts and ordered.

The pizza arrived and she set it on her kitchen table. He picked it up and put it on the coffee table next to the couch then pulled them both down on the couch, with her between his legs.

Would he feed her here on land?

"Yes," he said, reading her thoughts. He opened the box and lifted out the slice with the most anchovies. "Is way of sea forms."

She remembered the times she'd been at restaurants with Mike and Cerissa. She loved it when he fed her bites from his plate and ate mostly finger food. Did she tell Mike about the custom of sea forms? Had he been under the waves?

He held the corner of the pizza to her lips. "No, he has not been under the waves. This I ask."

She chewed the salty, cheesy pizza. As the flavors exploded on her tongue, she wondered if he would always know what she was thinking.

"Yes," he said smugly.

"How did you know I would want the piece with the most anchovies?" she said. "I never eat them."

"We are joined," he said, as if that explained everything. Somehow, it did. "When we are in great hall, at times you will take your own food."

He held the slice to her lips and she took another bite, leaving sauce at the corner of her mouth. "Napkins are on the table," she said, wiggling away from him.

He pulled her back and licked off the bit of sauce.

Heat flooded her core. Holy hell.

Ping. She had a text.

It was from her father. His plane landed, he'd caught a shuttle to her mother's hotel and was able to get an extra key to her mother's room from the front desk.

Her dad was a police captain and he must have used his cop-like manner to get the key. Hotel employees were paid to protect a guest's privacy. But when Captain Robert Paxton wanted action or answers, he got them.

Holy shit.

What would he make of Ethan? Her mother would tell him they were married as soon as she woke up. She needed answers from Ethan and they had to get their stories straight.

"Ethan, we have to talk," she said before he fed her the rest of the slice.

She scrambled out from between his legs so she could see his face. He swallowed his bite of pizza and watched her intently. She laced her fingers through his and smiled nervously.

"Your message has you upset," he said.

"My dad, sire, is here with Mom."

He squeezed her had. "This is not good?"

"It is and it isn't. He's a cop, a police detective. He investigates crimes. And he's good at it."

He smirked. "Like *Hawaii 5-O?*"

"W—what?" she sputtered. "You watch TV in the Garnet City?"

"Land dweller's transmission comes through crystals. I don't watch much. Mostly information from land forms who sit behind tables."

"News shows?" she said.

He reached for another slice of pizza and held it to her lips. She took a big bite.

"There is much hate and hurting among land forms," he said, taking a bite of pizza.

She sighed. "I know. I write about it. If it bleeds, it leads."

He looked puzzled.

"Violence and hate makes news. That's what Dad and other police try to stop. And the good things that happen, we don't report. But back to Dad, he will know you are different."

Seemingly unconcerned, he pulled her back into his lap and nuzzled her neck.

"We are different, darling."

"What do I say your job is?"

He slid his hands under her T-shirt and cupped her breasts.

Holy crap. She had been braless in the newsroom. Luckily, Cheryl didn't spare her a glance. But had Glenn noticed?

She pushed that thought out of her mind. She had bigger things to worry about. "We have to get our stories straight before we see dad."

He lifted her shirt and laved first one nipple then the other. "My scribe and her stories."

She moaned and he eased her down on the cushions. She slid her hands under his stretchy shirt and held onto his shoulders. "I mean it, Ethan, he won't stop asking until he gets answers." And maybe not even then.

"I protect places for life forms in sea," he said.

"So we'll say you're a marine biologist."

He moved a finger to her sensitive nub as his mouth found her nipple. She came instantly, her fingernails digging into his skin. He yanked her shorts down, and his, and sank into her slick channel.

She felt complete and reveled in his fullness.

"My worst interview ever," she said, lifting his shirt so she could suck on his flat nipples. "You distract me."

He shuddered and surged into her. She yanked his shorts down farther and caressed his fine ass.

He increased the tempo. As she hung on the precipice, he slowed. She dug her nails into his back in frustration.

"Ethan, please."

His lips quirked into a smile. "You said I am worst."

"Payback?" She palmed his scrotum and clenched her inner muscle around him. He shut his eyes.

"You know you are the only one I've joined with," she said. "I meant talking. Like on TV news."

She moved her hand to her sex but he stopped her.

"Mine," he growled.

He thrust into her, hitting her G-spot, and pressed down on her clit. She went into orbit as he emptied himself inside her.

When she came back to herself, she was wedged against him on the couch, her head pillowed on his chest.

He smoothed her hair away from her face. "You are with me again," he said, smoothing her hair back from her face.

She caressed the golden skin on his chest. "I always want you," she said.

He trailed her hand to her waist, then her hips.

Crap. Tension shot through her. He sat up, sat her on his lap, then stood, wrapping her legs around his waist and carried her to the bathroom. He put her in the bath tub and turned on the water. When the tub was filled, he got in and pulled her against his chest. She felt the familiar tingling and giggled when her tail unfurled. He laughed as he also took sea form, tugging on her necklace to settle it between her breasts.

"We talk now," he said. He held her breasts in his hands. "I always want you," he murmured against her ear.

Focus. She had to focus. "So we tell my parents you're a marine biologist who also studies oceanographic patterns."

Chapter 5

He kissed her neck, finding the spot near her ear that made her shiver with desire, then tweaked her nipples.

"You're distracting me," she said, although she made no move to stop him.

A fierce wave of possessiveness gripped him. "Mine, Becca."

"Cerissa said we eloped, so Mom will tell Dad as soon as she opens her eyes. He won't like it."

He had to explain to her that he couldn't live on land indefinitely, although it seemed Cerissa was doing so. If Becca stayed with him in the Garnet City, and took her full sea form, she would only be able to come ashore for three earth rotations at a time. How did Cerissa survive on land without the pure essence of water only found under the tides? Was she partly land form?

"We'll say you got your doctorate at the University of Hawaii and we eloped two weeks ago," she said. "I'll say my ring is getting sized and you can't wear one because of your work."

She twisted around and took his face in her hands. She looked worried. "The eating thing. You can't feed me in front of my parents. It isn't done. We use knives and forks to eat."

"A knife, after food is prepared?" It made no sense. Many customs of land forms baffled him. Why was she so worried about rings and why did land forms feel the need to wear metal on their hands?

"What is fork?" he said.

She spread her fingers out. "A utensil we eat with. We spear the food off the plate and bring it to our mouths." She rubbed her temples. "Let me suggest food to you. I'll choose things we eat with our hands, like hamburgers and sandwiches."

He covered her soft lips with his fingers. "I—we—may stay on land for three earth rotations."

She kissed his fingers and pulled them away from her mouth. "Then, what?"

"We return together through portal. As new sea form, you have chance to do so but we must go through portal together. Or I must make journey through seas. If you stay, I may not use the portal. Sea forms may only do so four times during earth revolution."

She swallowed hard. "You're saying you used your chance. And if I don't go back with you in three days, you'll have to swim back alone."

Tears fell down her cheeks. How could he ask her to leave her family and everything she knew on land to be with him?

He only knew he needed her as he needed the essence of pure water.

"If I don't go with you, when would I see you again?" she said.

"Winter solstice," he said.

Free will, she had to be with him by free will. It was written in the sacred laws. Her spirit he loved so much would wither if life in the Garnet City was not a choice she made with joy and love.

And Lovion and his minions were no doubt monitoring this talk through the crystals.

"But we could come on land to see my parents four times a year?" she said.

He gently wiped the wetness on her cheeks. "As you learn your fins as a mature sea form, you will not age like land forms."

She traced lazy circles on his chest. He sucked in a breath. Did she know what her touch did to him?

"How long do sea forms live?" she said.

"Hundreds of earth revolutions, unless we perish in the depths," he said.

She rubbed her stomach. "I need to take a pregnancy test," she said. She fluttered her tail. "You have to change me, us, back."

He lifted her out of the bathtub so she landed on her backside beside the tub. When her beautiful legs returned, she walked to a compartment that held clothing. He let the water drain from the tub and took his land form.

"Crap. None of my shoes fit. Something's wrong with my feet."

He couldn't take his eyes from her soft skin, glistening with moisture. "Darling, as you fully take sea form, you will wear nothing in Garnet City," he said. "Sea forms do not need to cover feet."

She put on a short robe-type garment that left her shoulders and legs below her knees bare.

She shuddered. "Nothing?" she said, "Ever?"

He took hold of her waist and pulled her into his arms. Her cheek rested against his chest. "I will want you wearing nothing in our chamber."

She slipped her feet into the footwear Cerissa gave her. She found the shirt and shorts he had worn before and held them out to him. "Come with?"

She looked frightened. He donned the garments, sheathing the knife under the clothing, and stepped into the footwear. She held out her hand and led him outside to her Corolla.

She drove a short distance to a small building and said he should wait for him in the Corolla but he refused. He couldn't bear to let her out of his sight. He kept hold of her hand, only letting it go when she opened a satchel to swipe a card across a machine. The land form who faced them put the box Becca selected in plastic with a small bit of paper.

Land form plastic. It was ruining the seas.

"Don't need this," he snarled, taking the box and paper from the plastic and handing it back to the land form. He tugged Becca back to the Corolla.

"What's wrong, Ethan?"

"Land forms ruin seas with plastic," he said, instantly regretting his angry tone when her lip trembled. He pulled her against his chest. "Lovion sire male who perish on mission to restore reef damaged by plastic." He held her until she pulled away.

She opened the doors to her vehicle. "So he hates people—land forms—on principle, not just me in particular," she said.

He saw she was seated safely before he folded his legs inside. "He also want males to join with sea forms from cities in Alliance," he said.

She sighed and stopped her car inside painted lines outside the building where she lived. He laced their fingers together and they went inside.

He punched the buttons on the machine that carried them up to the level where she lived and she put a metal piece in the door and turned around the device to open the door.

"You learn fast," she said. "The girls, females, that did my hair said you learned English after you saw me in the crystals."

She set the box she'd procured on the large round table. "How long ago was that?"

He pulled her into his arms and tugged on her necklace. "Time is different under the tides."

ဢၢ

He took hold of her chin and she stared into the depths of his turquoise eyes. He was impossibly handsome and she felt so ordinary. "You know everything about us. We know nothing about you," she said.

"Becca, we are the same."

She welled up, again. What was wrong with her? She never cried. She remembered the pregnancy test.

"I have to pee," she said, taking the box into the bathroom. She'd splurged on the test that gave instant results.

It was positive. She was pregnant. She put the strip and box in the wicker basket she used for trash. She'd hide it before her parents came. He'd turned on her TV and stared at it, frowning.

"Ethan?" He came to her side, instantly. "I—we—are pregnant."

He smiled, lifted her into his arms as if she weighed nothing, and carried her to the couch, sitting so she was settled between his legs.

He likes this position, she thought.

He massaged her neck and shoulders, releasing knots of tension. "Already, I know this," he said.

To her horror, she burst into tears. "How does it work in the Garnet City? How does any of it work?"

He wrapped her tightly in his arms and sang her name until she calmed. "I will show you," he said.

The doorbell rang. "Rebecca?" her mother called out.

Becca sprang off the couch. Was her father with her? Had she taken her meds? How had she gotten into the building without getting buzzed inside? She straightened her clothes and looked through the peephole.

Her dad was there. He didn't look happy.

Ethan stood behind her and took hold of her waist. "Breathe, Becca," he said and tugged on her necklace.

"Remember our stories," she whispered.

"Becs? You okay," her father said.

With a sweaty hand, she opened the door. Her mother's color was off. Becca looked at her father. He mouthed "No meds."

Ethan moved them aside. "Come in," she said.

Ethan let her go and her father swept her into his arms and hugged her. "Hey, baby girl."

Her mother stepped to Ethan and hugged him. Her father let her go and gave him the Captain Rob once over.

Ethan met her father's regard and put his hands on her shoulders. Some of her high school dates had cowered under her father's scrutiny.

"Dad, this is Ethan."

She tried to send Ethan the thought to shake her father's hand, with an image of what that was. She felt like she could puke with nerves.

Ethan extended his hand.

She expelled a breath she'd been holding.

"Rob," her dad said, curtly as he took Ethan's hand.

"Sit down," Becca said. "How are you feeling, Mom?"

Her mother shook her head and made a face. "They switched up my meds."

"Is there a pharmacy close?" her dad said.

She gave him the address and phone number of the one they'd just been to from the receipt she'd stuffed in her pocket, and he stepped into the kitchen and called her mom's doctor. Her mother looked at her dad and frowned.

"I'll just be a sec," her mother said, going into the bathroom.

Crap.

The pregnancy test.

Her mother squealed behind the closed door.

"Janet?" Her father opened the bathroom door.

Becca shook with nerves. Ethan massaged her shoulders and crooned her name.

"Becs is pregnant," her mother said. She put her hands on Rob's shoulders and jumped up and down. "We're going to be Nana and Papa."

Becca smiled at her mother's joy. Her mother ran to her and folded her into her arms. "My smart, beautiful girl is going to be a mother." She kissed her cheek and smoothed her hair back from her face like she did when Becca was a little girl. "You're going to be wonderful. I can't wait."

Becca struggled not to cry. How could she leave her parents to go with Ethan to the Garnet City?

Her dad motioned for Ethan to join him at the kitchen table. Ethan squeezed her shoulder and left her.

Her father pulled a wad of cash from his wallet and held it toward Becca. "Take your mom to the beach then to the drug store." Rob said. "Her script will be ready in an hour."

Shit. She didn't want to leave Ethan alone with her father while he was in full detective mode. But Rob hadn't it phrased it as a question.

She moved toward Ethan. He smiled and nodded. "Be with your mother," he said.

Reluctantly, she grabbed her keys and purse. "Let's go, Mom."

Her mother chattered non-stop on the short drive to the beach and didn't even mention the broken car window. The waves were up and they watched the surfers.

"Let's stick our feet in," her mother said, running to

the water's edge before she could stop her. Her mom waded in up to her knees, uncaring that she soaked the bottoms of her capris shorts.

Becca felt terrified of stepping into the vast ocean without Ethan and slipping into sea form. "Mom, come back."

Her mom laughed when a wave crested, drenching her, and screamed when it dragged her into deeper water.

Becca dropped her car keys onto a bench and dove in, felt the familiar tingling. She barely had time to pull her shorts off and slip them over her arm before her tail unfurled. Her head was above water but, fighting panic, she struggled to breathe. As she swam out to her mother, she felt something solid and slippery against her arm.

"Squawk."

It was Nudge.

"Oooh, a dolphin," her mother said as she treaded water. Becca held tight to the dolphin's fin as Nudge swam toward her mother.

The surfers were a long way off but a couple of families on the beach seemed to be watching them. Had they heard what her mother said about a dolphin over the waves?

"Shhhh, Mom. We want to keep Nudge safe," she said.

"Nudge?" her mother said. The dolphin let her mother stroke her while Becca tried her best to hide her tail from her mother and Nudge from the people on the beach.

"Becs, this is amazing," her mother said, beaming. "We're swimming with a dolphin. And you know its name."

Her smile faded and her lip trembled.

"What is it, Mom?"

"Nobody will believe me, or you. They'll think you're sick like I am, and I know you aren't."

A wave crested. Becca grabbed her mother's hand as it propelled them toward the shallows. Nudge swam back into deeper water.

Her mother gasped. "Becca?" She looked down. They were in shallow water and her tail glittered in shades of crimson and turquoise.

"The same shade as your necklace" her mother murmured, trembling. "But it's a delusion. It must be."

Becca couldn't, wouldn't, make her mother suffer.

"It isn't, Mom, I promise. Ethan is the same. And I'm going to live with him under the waves."

Crap. She sounded delusional. Was she? Forcing herself to focus on the problem at hand, she looked toward the families on the beach.

"Mom, you have to help me. Nobody can see me like this. Let me put my tail over your legs so it's out of the water, but nobody can see. When I dry out, I'll run for shore. Hopefully we won't get drenched again."

"Give me your shorts, Becs," her mother said. "We'll have to work fast."

Her mother's color looked better and she seemed

completely present and lucid. Maybe she was over medicated?

"Can you come back and visit after you go with Ethan? We'll all miss you," her mother said.

"I'm not close to Keith and Cara, Mom. And my friends from college are scattered, and I'm sad we're losing touch, but we are. And I haven't made many friends here, yet. It's you and Dad." Her voice cracked with emotion.

Her mother squeezed her hand. A little boy and his mother waded into the water, coming closer and closer.

Shit oh shit oh shit.

"Squawk." Nudge popped her head out of the water and everyone on the beach splashed into the water to get near the dolphin, ignoring Becca.

She felt the familiar tingle.

"Your legs, Becs," her mother said. Her mother pulled her shorts over her feet and up her legs as she did when Becca was five years old.

Becca ran for shore. Her mother stayed in the shallows watching the group that hoped to see Nudge then she waded to shore. "The dolphin is safe, I think," her mother said, looking sad and pale again. "Your guardian dolphin, huh?"

"Let's go, Mom. I'm okay." Becca picked up her car keys off the bench, which thankfully nobody had taken.

"You are." Her mom squeezed her hand. "I'll miss you so much."

Becca got her purse out of the trunk and bundled her mother into her car.

They picked up the meds at the drive-thru window. Her mother was quiet on the short ride back. Becca looked at her building with a sense of foreboding. She shouldn't have left Ethan with her father.

Tension cracked through the air when Becca opened the door. Her father looked furious.

She handed the meds to her mom and grabbed Ethan's hand. "Could you help me?" she said.

He nodded and she dragged him out of the apartment and inside the elevator before her father could stop them. She didn't realize she was shaking until he took her into his arms. He felt like heaven and home. The elevator opened and he threaded his fingers through hers. They walked to the parking lot and sat in her car.

He pulled her over the console and onto his lap. "My mother knows," she said. "She went into the water. A wave crested. I went in after her and she saw my sea form. Nudge created a diversion."

He stroked her hair. It was sticky from salt water. "You did not fear the sea."

"I did. But I forgot about it when Mom washed out to sea. What happened with Dad?"

"I do not have second name as you do and it angered him."

Oh shit oh shit oh shit. How could she have been so stupid not to think of that?

"You will miss them?" he said.

"Yes," she said, staring at her building.

Chapter 6

Her father burst out the door, scanned the lot, then and stalked toward them.

Crap.

"A word, Rebecca," her dad said. "Leave us, Ethan, whoever the hell you are."

"Becca?" Ethan didn't take his eyes off her face, not sparing her father a glance.

"Go ahead." She sighed. "Is Mom awake to buzz him in?"

Her dad nodded.

She opened the car door and stood up to let Ethan out.

Her father noticed the smashed out window. "What the hell is this?"

"Smash and grab," she said. "But nothing was inside."

Ethan stared into her eyes. She loved him so much. He smiled at her. Had he read her thoughts? His words filled her head. *We are twin flames. Forever, it is done.* He squeezed her shoulder and left them.

Her father rubbed his forehead, which meant he was pissed.

But this was her life. It was time for her to take charge of it.

"He doesn't have a last name, Becca," he yelled. "Who doesn't tell their wife's father their last name?" He didn't give her a chance to answer. "Someone with something to hide, that's who."

He would hammer her until she told him the truth. She had to spin something. "He didn't grow up in the states," she said.

He put his hands on the hood of the car. "No shit."

"W-we are going to live offshore," she said.

He erupted. "Like hell. You're giving up your job?"

"I'll get another one," she said. Her heart was racing and she was sweating. She'd never been this firm with her father. She sat down on the car seat. "I love him, Dad. And he loves me."

"How will you live?" he yelled.

"He's a marine biologist."

"Hmmmph. Where are you going?"

"They call it Garnet City. Not sure if there's cell service."

He clenched his hands into fists. "So you're pregnant and you think you are going to live offshore where nobody can reach you. What if it doesn't work out? He doesn't have a fucking last name."

He was yelling and people stared.

"He sings," she said, in an effort to calm him down. "He tried it professionally and he legally changed his name." Her lie sounded pathetic. And her dad always knew when she lied.

"The man was born with a last name," her father made no attempt to lower his voice, uncaring of the people in the parking lot looking them.

"He wasn't born here and it is hard to pronounce and spell," she said. It was true. He could have a surname in language of the sea forms. "It's an island language, near Guam."

A police cruiser pulled up and a male officer about her age stepped out. "Is everything okay, miss?"

Was it? She felt weak and nauseated. How far would her father take this? Ethan strode across the parking lot. The officer waited for her to answer.

She held her hand out to Ethan. He took it and pulled her into the crook of his arm. "Yes, my father and I were arguing loudly. I'm sorry if we were disturbing anyone. This is my husband. My father doesn't approve."

Her father told the officer he served on the Fort Wayne PD. The officer nodded curtly.

"She's unwell, she must take food," Ethan said.

"Do you feel safe?" the officer said.

She said she did, although she shook with nerves. Ethan said they had to leave for the Garnet City in two days. How would she slip away from the watchful eye of her dad?

The officer nodded and Ethan led her toward the building.

"My wife is upstairs," her father said. "She's resting."

"Do you feel safe if he comes with you, Miss?" the officer said.

Ethan turned her around, keeping firm hold of her waist. She looked at the man who was her rock her entire life that she would turn her back on to be with the man she loved.

"Yes," she said.

"Thank-you for doing your job," her dad told the officer.

Her mother was awake and obviously medicated when they got back upstairs. Becca held out her car keys. "Take Mom back to your hotel."

"I got a rental," he said.

Her mother got to her feet, hugged Becca, and whispered in her ear, "I took the damn pills so he'd keep an eye on me. Do what you have to."

Louder she told Becca she loved her and released her.

Her father took her mother's arm and they left.

Becca sank down on the couch, exhausted. "We have to leave before they come back," she said.

He opened her refrigerator and pulled out a carton of eggs. "First, you must take food."

She watched in amazement as he found her one frying pan in a cabinet, put it on the stove, turned on the burner, and cracked the eggs in the pan. "You know how to cook?" she said.

He fished a spatula out of her silverware drawer and grinned. "TV. *Hawaii 5-0.*"

He expertly cracked all the eggs in the carton into the pan and dumped the shells in her sink.

Unable to resist, she went to him and wrapped her arms around his lean, hard body. "You are amazing," she said.

The eggs were done and he moved the pan off the burner. She turned the knob off and pulled a plate out of the cupboard. He put the eggs on the plate with the spatula.

Before she could grab a fork, he took the plate to the coffee table, sat down on the couch, and patted the spot next to him. Was he going to feed her scrambled eggs by hand?

He did. It was messy. He cleaned her up with his mouth and she dissolved into a fit of giggles.

She ate half the plate, then waved him off, scooped the eggs on her fingers and brought it to his lips. He turned his face so some of the eggs landed on his cheek. She licked them off.

He groaned and rolled her underneath him. She rubbed against his erection. He pulled her damp shorts off her and thrust inside her. She was wet for him.

"Look at me, Becca."

His eyes blazed silver. She caressed his firm, smooth jawline. He withdrew, then thrust again, hitting all her nerve endings. She moaned, never taking her eyes from his face.

She gripped his tight, hard ass. "I want you so much," she said.

He pumped faster. "As I want you."

She came apart in his arms. He covered her mouth as she came, screaming his name before he emptied himself inside her.

When she came back to herself, she felt frightened. "We have to leave, Ethan, my father—"

"He loves you," he said, stroking her hair back from her face.

"I told him we were going to live off shore and he went ballistic."

He looked puzzled.

"He lost his temper," she said. "He'll try to stop me—us. I know it."

He eased out of her and cupped her face in his hands. "You are sure?"

Leaving her parents was breaking her heart, but Ethan *was* her heart. "Yes," she said. "Forever, it is done."

He claimed her mouth in a hard, possessive kiss that went on forever. When he lifted his mouth, she reluctantly squirmed away from him. She rinsed the egg shells down the garbage disposal, threw out all the perishable food in her fridge, and dumped the garbage down the chute.

Ethan turned on her TV and flipped through the channels, frowning.

She sent Cheryl an email, resigning from her job, saying she had a family emergency and resisted the urge to tell her she was a flat-out bitch of a boss. Next, she emailed her landlord that she wouldn't be renewing her lease, which was up next month and to let Mike inside to clear out her stuff. Last she called Mike.

It went to his voicemail. She said she was leaving with Ethan, wished him the best with Cerissa, asked him to take or trash the stuff in her apartment, and gave him her landlord's contact info.

"I'm ready," she said. "What do we do?"

Ethan turned off the TV. "There is a place called Waimea."

"Should I take anything?"

He tugged on her necklace and grinned. "Only me."

She grabbed her purse and car keys and shut the door behind them. She'd been so focused on her job and her deadlines, she'd never gotten around to exploring what was called the Grand Canyon of the Pacific in the ten months she lived on Kauai. What a waste.

As she drove through the Waimea State Park entrance, her cell phone pinged. She'd forgotten she had it in her purse. They pulled into a spot by the visitor's center and she pulled it out.

It was a text from her father. *Your mother's cell phone says you're at Waimea Canyon. We're right behind you.*

Crap.

She'd forgotten about the app she and her mother had set up.

She texted back *OK.* "We have to hurry," she said.

ᏉᎤᏉ

Did she know she was weeping? She drew stares from the land forms near them. He put his hands on her shoulders and drew her back against him. "Sad news," he said when a land form wearing shorts and a head adornment came near.

She wiped the wetness from her cheeks and turned to him. "Where to?"

"This way." He took her hand, walked along the long path to the ancient place, and waited for the other land forms to pass. "Here." He squeezed her hand and led her off the marked path, through rough terrain to the entrance to the portal. "You must enter first. And you must keep your hands on me."

"Becca?" Her mother's voice called out. "They're over there, Rob."

Becca grabbed both of his hands. "Go first, Ethan."

He pulled her behind him. Something held her back. She gripped his hands, but her mother took hold of her. "What are you doing?" she said.

"What are you thinking going off the path," Rob said. He held Becca's mother by her arm. "There are signs posted."

"Let go, Mom," Becca said.

But it was too late.

Chapter 7

Because they were touching, all four of them hurled through the portal and the vortex. They scrambled from the sacred passage to the outskirts of the Garnet City. "This is one hell of a dream," Rob said.

Ethan pointed to the channel. "Darling, we need essence of pure water and to take sea form." He took off his shorts, shirt, and foot coverings.

Rob turned Janet away from them. "Holy hell."

Becca disrobed. Ethan dropped her into the narrow channel and jumped in after her.

She sighed as he pressed his mouth to hers. He wanted nothing more than to join with her on the path to the city.

But it was not possible with her sire at her side. Her tail unfurled. She looked worried and frightened. "What will happen? They—we—are in danger, right?"

He kissed her again, not caring if her sire saw their passion. He lifted his lips. "You are home. We are home. We must speak to the elders, tell them this was not what we want."

"Squawk." Janet squealed. Becca's dolphin popped her head out of the channel. "It's your dolphin, Becs," her mother said, bending down to touch the dolphin.

Rob looked into the channel. "Are we under the ocean?"

Becca fluttered her tail. "See, Dad."

Her father gasped for breath and clutched his chest. Becca screamed.

"Rob, breathe," Janet said, standing up to put her arms round him. "I tried to tell you, but you just thought I was wacko."

Ethan stopped Becca as she tried to pull herself out of the water. "We must keep sea form after bridging time and space." He held her against him. "You are altered. Like me."

Rob put his hands on his wife's shoulders, then ran his fingers over the veins of red that ran through the wall of minerals that led to the Garnet City. "Your kind, I'm guessing they won't be happy to see us," he said.

"They welcome Becca," Ethan said.

"Ethan's parents are very kind," Becca said.

Ethan palmed her breasts under the water. He loved her so much. What would the Ruling Council do when they learned his twin flame's parents had crashed through the portal? They would separate them from the sea forms and Becca until healers were certain they posed no threat, although sea forms were thought to be immune from land form disease.

"Ethan?" Lara and Thorion swam toward them. Both bristled with tension. Thorion spoke in the language of the sea forms and told him Lovion had convinced the Ruling Council that Becca had deliberately allowed her parents to burst through the portal. This was in violation of dictates of all the cities in alliance under the riptides.

Thorion said in halting English that both Becca and he would face charges of treason unless Becca's parents immediately returned to land. Rob and Janet's minds would be altered so they had no memory of the journey.

Speaking in English, Lara said that, because of Janet's illness, this posed a risk that her condition would worsen. "Our healers would do what they can. We are more advanced than land forms," she said to Becca's parents. She turned to Ethan. "If Becca returns with them, and you say you knew nothing of their intent, she may not return to Garnet City. You would face no charges, then, my son."

"I've ruined everything," Janet wept. "We love you,

that's all." She crumpled to the ground and leaned toward the channel, taking Becca in her arms. Becca wept as her heart was breaking.

"What happens if Becca stays? Will she face charges?" her father said. Thorion hauled himself out of the water. Janet and Becca averted her eyes as he took land form.

"Charges are that breach is deliberate to harm sea forms," he said." If Becca stays, she face charge of treason. Ethan would face lesser charge of accomplice."

"She will stay," Ethan said. "Charges stupid. Three land forms not mount an attack on Garnet City. Is not possible."

"Lovion convincing to Elder Council," Lara said.

Ethan bellowed in rage then chanted ancient words of curse and hated toward Lovion.

"Stop," Lara said. "If harm comes to him and someone heard you—"

He looked at the tear-stained faces of Lara, Becca, and her mother. Becca shivered in his arms, although the channel was tepid.

"What is the penalty for treason?" Rob said.

"She would cease to draw breath," Thorion said.

"I will not let that happen," Ethan said.

"We will not let that happen," her father said. "I'm better to you here. I can help you. I've testified in court more times than I can count, and this asshole that's behind this—shit, I can help you shut him down." He clenched his hands into fists. "We'll leave you after Becs is safe. I know my daughter. She won't come back with us, not without you. It would be akin to pleading guilty and she won't do that."

Becca nodded.

"I'm good at investigating things," her father said. "My daughter stands a better chance if we stay."

Ethan wrapped Becca in his arms. She wound her arms around his neck and their tails intertwined. Something poked him in the stomach.

Becca gasped. "The baby moved." She said. "But I'm barely pregnant. It's too soon."

Lara put her hand on Becca's shoulder. "Is different for sea forms. The healers will speak of this."

Becca's eyes blazed gray like the sea on a stormy day. "He likes the idea," she said. "Mom and Dad should stay to see us through this."

Squawk.

The dolphin lifted its head and smiled.

Becca laughed. "See? Nudge agrees."

Did she know he would agree to anything when she laughed like that or that her sire would have very little freedom to investigate?

"Forgive my bluntness, but you have to play offense, not defense. This Lovion character, you need to attack him, not physically, although I'd like to pound my fists into his face."

Lara spoke in the language of the sea forms, repeating what Rob said so his sire had clear understanding.

"You hold a position of power here," Rob said.

"One seat on Ruling Council, suspended, pending outcome of charges," Thorion said.

Two young sea forms approached, carrying white robes for Lara and Thorion and beige garments, denoting low rank, for Rob and Janet, although they wouldn't realize that. Ethan's parents set them up in chambers in the outer reaches of the Garnet City under guard.

He and Becca returned to their chamber in the city— for now. They were innocent of the bogus charges and would act as such. They took land form and he summoned food and drink for them, which would have awaited them if not for Lovion's nonsense. Servers brought it and he filled a crystal goblet of Becca's favorite amber liquid and held it to her lips. She drank it all and he filled it again. "Drink, darling," he said.

She sat on the bed and finished the goblet.

He filled a flat shell with lobster, cod, and sea vegetables and took it to the bed. He removed her shirt and settled her between his legs and held a morsel of lobster in a savory sauce to her lips. She chewed it and sucked the sauce from his fingers which made his cock hard as the crystal goblet.

She noticed and ran her hand up and down over his hard length.

"I'm hungry for you, too," she said. "It seems like forever since we joined."

He moved the food aside and rolled her beneath him and feasted on her nipple as he tweaked its twin. He slid his finger inside her sex.

She was wet for him. He teased her sensitive bud of nerves with his thumb then moved his loin cloth aside and thrust inside her.

She moaned and scored her nails across his shoulders. "This part is so easy," she said, clenching her muscles around him. He nearly spilled his seed.

He eased out of her. "Becca. I will spill my seed as I did when I was still learning my fins."

"I'm afraid," she whispered.

He plunged back into her slick, wet channel. He wanted to savor her, bring her to the edge until she could only think of him, and how he would pleasure her until they ceased to draw breath. He pulled out and thrust harder, hitting the back of her womb.

"There's just this, and us, darling. Forever, it is done."

He pumped into her and pulled on her nipple. When she came screaming his name, he filled her with his seed. He stayed buried inside her, stroking her hair. "We will fix this. Lovion is…how you say it?…toast."

She laughed. It sounded like goblets clinking together.

⟡⟡⟡

Ethan argued with males in long robes. His father

stood next to him and put his hands on his son's shoulders. Ethan turned away from the men in the robes and came to her. She wore a long white robe like his that touched the ground. "We must leave you," he said. "They mean to question you."

She grasped his shoulders. "But I don't speak your language. How will I make them understand?"

Her father came into the chamber wearing a beige robe that reached to his knees. Two sea forms in royal blue robes flanked him. His guards?

"Don't show fear," her father said. "You've done nothing wrong."

Lara entered the chamber.

"She has the best skill with English of all in Garnet City," Ethan said.

Becca slid her hands around Ethan's neck and kissed him as if they were alone, drawing strength from their connection. She stepped back and smiled. "I am also good with words. I'll be fine."

He pulled on her necklace. "What is fine?"

She caressed his cheek. "Us, we are fine."

He pressed a kiss to her palm. "Yes," he said, fingering her necklace and tugging on her braid that hung over one shoulder. He and Thorion left the chamber. She straightened her spine. She'd covered wily city politics and dealt with a mean-spirited boss for months.

She was sick of feeling bullied and afraid. "I worked with Cheryl. I can do this."

"That's my girl," her father said.

Lara asked that she explain what happened at Waimea.

Without preamble, she told them what happened as if she were reporting it for a news story.

Lara asked her father the same question. He said they wanted to be near Becca and Ethan because they were worried about her. An elder spoke a few words.

Lara nodded and answered in the language of the sea forms. She turned to them. "I said that worry is concern for well-being. That is correct?"

Becca and her father nodded.

"Why was this worry?" Lara said.

"We wanted to be sure Becca was safe," her father said. "Things about Ethan raised our worry. He had no surname. Humans take a family name as well as a given name." He rubbed his hands together. "I am Robert Paxton, or Captain Paxton. I hold rank as one who enforces human laws. A woman takes a surname, too. She takes her father's surname until she is married, then she most times takes her husband's, mate's name. Becca is Rebecca Paxton. Ethan was only Ethan. People who break laws don't use their surnames or use false ones so that those who enforce the laws can't find them."

Lara spoke at length to the elders. They didn't look at her as they left the chamber.

Lara kept her distance from Becca. "I may not speak of the elder's discourse."

Two male sea forms came into the chamber and moved toward her father. "My escorts?" he said.

Lara nodded.

"May I embrace my daughter before I leave?" he said.

Lara spoke a few words to the guards then nodded.

Her father hugged her tight. She fought back tears. She had to believe everything would be okay. They had done nothing they had believed to be wrong.

He let her go. "That's my girl," her father said. He turned to Lara. "This is what parents and children do when they greet one another or say goodbye."

Lara said something to the guards. Her father winked at Becca then followed the guards out.

"Are we permitted to speak?" Becca said.

"Not about charges." Lara said. She didn't move toward her.

"Where is Ethan?"

"Talking with Elder Council."

Becca swallowed hard. Lara's distance was unsettling. "Is my mother well?"

"She has not swallowed pellets she brought in her satchel. She had session with healers."

"Must I stay in this chamber?"

Lara sighed. "I will be with you until Ethan arrives."

Am I under guard? Becca felt violently ill and sank to her knees on the marble floor, taking deep breaths. "I am hungry. May I take food?"

Lara helped her to her feet and led her to an adjoining chamber with cushions on the floor. Becca sat down and Lara left. Her guards stood outside.

Ethan had held her in his arms in their chamber and assured her these charges would be deemed as nonsense. He'd been so sure. And now she was essentially being held in custody. So were her parents. Lara was distant. And Ethan was gone.

Her guards spoke with someone then left.

Lovion entered the chamber and stood over her.

Hell no. She got to her feet to look him in the eye, as his equal. Time to play offense. "You hate land forms," she said.

Lovion narrowed his eyes. They looked like chards of silver. "You encroach the seas and foul the land and air that sustains you."

"I and my parents and many others try not to do that," she said.

He sneered. "Most do," he said.

She bowed her head. Sea forms did this, she'd noticed, as a sign of respect for those who perished. "I am sorry for the losses you have suffered."

He continued as if she hadn't spoken. "If you and your sire and mother depart, the elders will not pursue charge for Ethan."

"We have done nothing wrong," she said.

"He is under guard and will remain so until Elder Council makes decision, unless you leave, of your choice."

Was he bluffing?

The baby kicked her hard. She put her hand over her stomach and smiled, which incensed Lovion.

His icy glare chilled her. "Your offspring is land form and will have lower rank. Lara is different with you, now, is she not?"

Becca struggled to look calm.

"Is because charges. Thorion is suspended from his duties on Ruling Council seat his ancestors hold since ancients were learning fins."

She gritted her teeth as he handed her a crystal prism.

"Ethan speaks with Mina," he said.

She peered through the crystal and felt woozy. Ethan had his hands on the shoulders of the female she took to be Mina, and he smiled at her.

"If you stay and elders dismiss charges against him, he will join with her so he has offspring wholly sea form to continue ruling line."

"No." The word slipped out before she could stop it.

"You see his way with her," he said. "You would be second wife if you stay."

Was Lovion lying?

Another image flickered through the crystal. This one was cloudy, but she could still make out Ethan's handsome face. He sat on a raised platform with other sea forms in the center of the group, the place of leadership. Mina was near him.

"This is his destiny, with Mina," he said.

Not her. "My baby—" She couldn't think, wouldn't think of the baby as their baby.

"He is safe."

He?

"He will not take sea form on land unless he is guided by native sea form," he said.

So he would never know his heritage or his father. But he would not face prejudice as he would here. She squared her shoulders and moved past him. "The portal, where is it?"

She would leave Ethan and the essence of who she was. Her parents would follow. Her baby would be safe. Ethan would fulfill his destiny as leader.

Numb, she followed Lovion through a series of winding passages until the came to a channel.

Squawk.

It was Nudge.

The baby kicked hard again. Becca knelt down to say goodbye to the dolphin and wrapped trembling arms around Nudge's neck. The dolphin lurched down, diving underwater. Becca hung tight to her fins. She heard Lovion's angry shout when the dolphin broke the surface. Becca took a deep breath and felt the familiar tingling then her tail unfurl. The loose robe was no barrier.

Nudge popped her head out of the water so she could draw breath. The dolphin didn't stop until they were in the great hall. Sea forms filled the space. Clear quartz crystals glittered throughout the room.

The Elder Council stood on the raised platform.

Becca hauled herself out of the channel, grateful for her robe, which was drying fast and only felt damp against her skin. Ethan stood near the Elder Council next to Mina.

Seething, Becca stood up. He wasn't touching Mina but she smiled at him, her heart in her eyes.

Becca scanned the room for her parents but she saw no beige robes.

"No," she screamed through the crowd. "I will not be your second wife. I will leave if she's who you want."

He didn't move. Why didn't he come to her? She bristled with rage.

"Why did you bring me here? I don't understand. You barged into my lunch date, spewing what I know now was garbage. Glenn liked me. You ruined it. Why?"

Murmurs of sympathy fluttered through the crowd, for her, the rejected, pathetic human.

Lara stood near Ethan speaking, likely translating for the Elder Council.

Still he stood there. "What do you mean second wife?" he said. His voice was strained.

She pointed to Mina. "I saw you both in the crystals. Lovion showed me before he took me to the portal. It was blurry, but I saw you. You touched her and smiled at her."

Her spate of energy, spurred by her anger, left her, evaporating like the water had from her robe. Ethan clenched his fists at his sides. Still he didn't come to her.

Drained, she sank to her knees and took deep breaths. She would not weep.

The elders spoke among themselves. She heard them say Lovion's name more than once. But she had no idea if they were pleased or angry from their faces or the tone of their voices.

She would leave on her own terms. She made her way through the crowd toward Ethan. The sea forms moved aside for her, saying words that sounded like approval.

She reached him and fingered her necklace, letting him see her love for him in her eyes for one last time. "Remove this necklace. I don't want it. Then you'll be free. I will leave."

"Free will," Lara said.

He bowed to Mina then stepped toward Becca, capturing her chin. A muscle twitched in his cheek. "Is this what you wish, to leave?"

She searched his turquoise gaze. "I will not stay and be your second wife."

"What is second wife?" he said.

"I will not share you with Mina," she said, casting off her pride.

His eyes widened in understanding then blazed silver. "You are my twin flame, the only one I join with. I tell you this before. You believe Lovion, not me?"

He set his lips in a hard line.

She brushed them with her fingertips. "Not at first. But you were touching her and smiling at her in the crystals. I felt like you did when Glenn touched me, remember? It's called being jealous. It made me stupid."

She covered the slight swell of her stomach with her hand. "He said something else. Our baby, offspring, would have lower rank—whatever that means—if I stayed here. I want the best for him. He said it's a boy."

Lara spoke rapidly in the language of the Garnet City. "Lovion was leading you to the portal, and you went willingly?" she asked Becca in English.

Was she still being questioned? "Yes," she said.

Ethan turned his back and stepped away from her.

Lara said words in the language of the sea forms and the crowd gasped.

That was it, then. Becca had taken her chance and failed. She'd willingly gone with Lovion to the portal. This violated a dictate in this foreign place, and Ethan didn't want her.

It was done. She tore her eyes from Ethan.

Squawk.

Nudge lifted her head from the channel.

Becca walked to the dolphin and, overcome with sadness, wrapped her arms around Nudge's neck. Once again, the dolphin pulled her into the water.

Grabbing onto her fins, Becca took a deep breath. *I love you so much.*

She sent her love to him before Nudge pulled her

under the water and she took sea form. Becca loved her sea-form tail. She would miss it.

Chapter 8

She meant to leave because she believed it was best for her offspring," the ranking matriarch said.

All sea forms awaited the verdict. Ethan's stomach churned. He had to stop Becca before she reached the portal. The elders nodded and the matriarch smiled. "Charges against you and Becca dissolved. Lovion will be tried for his treachery."

Becca's thoughts came to him. She loved him. He barely heard the last few words as he ripped off his robe and plunged into the channel. He swam toward the portal and hauled himself out of the water.

She wasn't there.

He bellowed a vile curse against Lovion then noticed the portal was light pink, rather than red, meaning it had not been used.

Where had her dolphin taken her?

When Becca recounted her story to the elders, he'd staggered away from her, feeling unworthy of her love because he had failed to protect her against Lovion's treachery. She must think he was angry that she had believed Lovion's lies and let him lead her to the portal.

I love you, Becca. Don't leave me.

Would his words reach her?

Where had she gone?

When they'd first entered the city, overcome with his need to possess her, he'd pulled her out of the channel and filled her until she came, screaming his name.

He dove into the channel and didn't surface until he reached that spot.

Squawk.

Nudge was there.

Becca stood on the path, weeping, looking toward the city. She put her hand on her stomach. "Not yet, Nudge, This is the last time I'll see this, and I need to be able to describe this glorious place."

Ethan loved her so much. He lifted himself out of the channel.

Startled, she whirled toward him as he took his land form. He took hold of her. He would never let her go.

"What would you say of this place?"

His heart thundered as she rested her cheek on his chest. "That the walls of the city that lies deep in the sea glow red like the embers in a fire," she said. "That I left my heart and soul here, with you."

He unfastened her gown and eased it off her shoulders. It pooled at her feet. He tugged on her necklace. "I would have searched all across your land for you, swimming through the seas for the rest of my existence." He lifted her face. "You are mine, Becca. You hold my heart. Mina is like sibling to me. She is joining with my fin mate. I wish her only well."

He kissed her gently, stroking her soft lips until she moaned and opened her mouth to deepen the kiss. Her tongue dueled with his and his cock hardened.

Putting his back against the wall, he lifted her, and wrapped her legs around his waist. He slid his finger into her slit.

She was wet for him. He groaned and circled her hidden pearl until she came, drenching his fingers.

Grunting, he thrust inside her, hitting the back of her womb. "You were made for me, darling. But you had to stay of your own free will. I couldn't touch you until the elders—"

He stopped speaking because his brain separated from his body as he pumped into her tight, wet channel. She screamed her release as his seed spurted inside her.

He eased them onto the path so she was in his lap.

"Thank God for you," she said, pressing her face into his neck.

"We must bring your dolphin mackerel as reward for bringing you back," he said. "I will find a net and teach you your fins."

Squawk. Her dolphin grinned, preening with pride.

"Ethan, my parents?"

He sighed. "Of course." He picked up her robe and dropped it over her head. "They are not far. The elders respect your sire as one who keeps order on land. Your mother—you will see."

She gasped and clutched his shoulders. "Ethan, my mother, is she ill? She hasn't taken her meds."

He pulled her to her feet. "No, darling. She is well. Our healers have helped her. It is good she came to Garnet City."

She sagged against him. He lifted her in his arms. She yawned. "I can walk," she said.

He chuckled.

ꜱꞓꜱꞓ

Autumn equinox a year later:

They stepped through the portal into Waimea Canyon where Becca's parents waited with clothes and a bag of gifts for their grandson.

Three months old by earth time, Gareth nursed

greedily, oblivious to his mother and grandmother weeping with joy.

Becca's mother, to the amazement of her healers on land, was not afflicted with her mental illness and didn't need the medicine since her visit to the Garnet City.

Becca's father averted his eyes from his daughter as she handed Gareth to Janet, who wrapped him in a cloth. Becca put on a gown-like garment that fell to her knees and left her arms bare. Ethan put on shorts and a shirt similar to what Rob wore.

A male in brown clothing walked toward them, frowning. "You can't be here."

Rob took a step toward him. "My grandson was hungry," he said. "We'll leave immediately."

They walked the short distance to a vehicle. Janet rummaged in a bag and fastened a white bit of what looked like paper on Gareth's bottom and pulled a shirt over his head inscribed with a heart shape and the word "grandma."

Then she fastened him into some sort of seat designed to contain small offspring, which displeased him. He screamed and Becca's lip trembled.

"Remove him," Ethan said.

"It's the law," Rob said.

"It keeps them safe," Becca said.

Gareth's face was red and he flailed his fists in rage.

Ethan took hold of Becca's waist and pulled her back against him, kissing her neck to calm her, although it made him hard. "Human rules?" he whispered into her ear.

"She spent three hundred dollars on baby stuff and you're staying three days," Rob said.

Janet didn't take her eyes off Gareth.

Becca went tense. "Dad?"

"No, Becs," he said. "Not manic, just happy."

Janet spoke a version of English to Gareth Ethan had never heard.

Reading his thoughts, Becca said, "It's baby talk. I do it too, just not as much."

She giggled. He loved that sound. He wanted to hear it for the rest of his existence. He let her go and she and her mother sat in the back with his screaming offspring and he sat in front. The journey was mercifully short to what Becca said was their time share.

They had devised a way for Becca to communicate with her parents from the depths when conditions were perfect. Becca said it was like Skype on land. They saw each other's faces, but the sound was delayed. Becca was sad for a time after each transmission, but she said it was normal to miss loved ones.

His mother was teaching Becca the language of the Garnet City, and she was learning quickly. She spoke both languages to Gareth. She watched her parents touch and speak to Gareth with such love and longing, his heart ached. Would she be able to leave them and return through the portal at the end of their time on land?

They arrived in front of a dwelling. Becca unfastened Gareth from what Janet said was a car seat and held him so his face was in full sun. She turned her face toward the sky. The breeze blew her hair into her face.

Did she long for the sun and wind on her skin in the depths?

The healers said she and Gareth could exist on land until the end of their existence. He—as wholly sea form—could not, according to the healers. He could walk on land for three earth rotations during what humans called their winter and summer solstices and spring and autumn equinoxes.

This was not the case with Cerissa, who had joined with Mike, the scribe Becca had worked with, who lived on land with him. The healers in the Garnet City could not explain this.

Ethan would bring Becca and his offspring on land as often as he could safely pass through the portal, during those times he could stay on land. He could not bear to leave her on land without him.

Chapter 9

Did she feel the same? Did she want to stay on land without him?

They sat on the porch in the sun and Gareth slurped from Becca's breast. Rob left them while Gareth nursed. Sea form offspring did not take solid food until one full revolution of the earth occurred since their birth.

The sun dipped lower in the sky. Gareth, sated, slept in Becca's arms. Janet asked if she could put him down, which Becca told him meant sleep. Janet scooped Gareth up and spoke nonsense English to him as she carried him indoors.

Ethan pulled Becca onto his lap to watch the sun slip

under the edge of the earth, lighting the sky like flame in shades of red and gold. She laid her head on his chest and sighed. His erection pressed into her backside and she wiggled against him.

Slipping his hand under her garment, he pressed his fingers against her sex. She was wet.

She was breathing hard. "Ethan."

He found the secret spot inside her and she rained her sweet nectar on his fingers. She turned her mouth into his neck to muffle her cries as he brought her to climax.

Rob bounded toward them. "Are you okay?" He glanced at them and winced. "Jeez, Becca." He went back indoors.

Ethan chuckled.

She covered her face with her hands. "He knows."

"We are...what you say?...busted," he said.

"Your English is getting better so fast," she said.

"I listen when you talk to Gareth," he said.

It was dark. Stars began to dot the sky like flecks of light reflected in the hall of crystals in the Garnet City.

She rubbed his arms. "I forget there are no bugs here. In Indiana, we'd be chewed up, even in September."

"Do you miss your home?"

"Lake Michigan looks like the ocean, although it's a ways from Fort Wayne. But home, Ethan, is in the depths with you."

He cradled her against him. Would she feel that way when she had to leave her parents?

Janet came outside. "Can I join you?"

Becca climbed off his lap. "Of course, Mom."

"Your dad is antsy and hungry."

Antsy?

"Would Gareth be okay if we went out to eat? You could nurse Gareth in the SUV if he gets fussy."

"Sure, Mom. I just need to do something with my hair."

"It's so shiny. You look amazing," Janet said.

Becca stood and put her arms around her mother. "Thanks, Mom, so do you."

They embraced until Rob walked outside, holding Gareth.

"The big guy woke up," he said. "He seems hungry. I changed him."

Changed?

Becca caught his eye and transmitted her thoughts. *He means his diaper.*

He smiled his thanks. His English language skills needed work. He had much to learn.

"I'll feed him out here," Becca said. Her mother let her go and went back indoors with Rob. Ethan sat next to her while Gareth took milk. Ethan did this whenever he was not busy with his duties on the Ruling Council. The electorate awarded him a seat after Lovion was removed.

Becca sighed as Gareth drank his fill. "You are perfect," she said.

He kissed her forehead, inhaling her cinnamon scent.

"My English words are not. But I will fix it." He took her chin and touched his lips to hers.

She kissed his jaw. "You have nothing to fix."

Gareth whimpered and Becca moved him to her other breast. "He drinks like he is starved." She frowned. "Do you think I have enough milk for him?"

He touched his forehead to hers. Her tender heart called to him. He would do anything to protect her and shield her from pain. "Yes, darling. The healers have assured us. Our offspring is greedy and craves being near you."

Gareth sucked for a bit then shut his eyes. Ethan took his sleeping offspring into his arms. "I know this feeling."

She pulled her gown up over her breasts and turned her face into his neck.

Janet and Rob sat down on a bench with cushions. "All set?" Janet said.

"My hair," Becca said. She stood up, went indoors, and came out a moment later. She'd secured it off her face, revealing the beautiful lines of her jaw and throat. She'd applied a red color to her lips and a dark color to her lashes. "You are beautiful as always," he said aloud, in the language of the sea forms.

Rob and Janet looked puzzled.

He inclined his head in a slight bow. "Forgive me. I said Becca is beautiful."

They smiled. He insisted that those in the Garnet city

who spoke English spoke it when Becca was near.

"Like her mother," Rob smiled.

"Could I hold him?" Janet said, staring at Gareth. "I know I'm hogging him."

Hogging?

"Of course," Ethan said. He handed his offspring to her and Rob guided them down steps to the vehicle.

Becca giggled. "Hogging means to crave being near someone."

He pinched her nipple. "Like this?"

She moaned, then covered her mouth with her hand.

'You okay?" Rob said.

She glared at Ethan. "Yes, Dad."

"I heard all the locals love Zeke's," Rob said.

"They do," Becca said.

Gareth howled when they fastened him in his contraption but fell asleep when the vehicle moved.

"We used to drive around so you'd stop crying," Janet said.

Rob laughed. "I used to see people driving around neighborhoods with infants in the backseat when I was on midnights."

"Turn here, Dad," Becca said.

They arrived and made their way through the crowd. Rob said he made a reservation. Becca and Janet put Gareth into another contraption with a handle on top and put him on the cushioned seat between them. Ethan sat next to Becca, in what Janet said was a booth, suddenly feeling a strong need to be within touching distance of Becca and Gareth.

This was the second place he saw Becca on land, taking a meal with the land form that touched her cheek. Was that why he was filled with tension?

A female handed then a long list of food.

"What's wrong?" Becca whispered.

Was his unease so obvious?

Janet whispered nonsense words to Gareth, and Rob stared at the carving of the female sea form that hung near a long table with many glass bottles filled with spirits, liquid meant to relax land forms. The healers said the spirits dulled land form senses and released inhibitions.

The female asked them what they wanted to drink.

"Get a Coke," Becca said. "You can't be on land and not try one."

A moment later the female placed their drinks on the table.

Ethan was reaching for his Coke when Becca grabbed his arm. "Mike and Cerissa are here." She laced her fingers through his. "They see us."

They stood and Mike maneuvered them to their table. Ethan gritted his teeth as Mike enfolded Becca in his arms.

Ethan bowed his head quickly to Cerissa. "I must ask you how you can remain here, on land." he said. "The healers say it is not possible for me."

Cerissa stepped closer to him. "The healers and elders in the Crystal City believe I am not wholly sea form. I was found on the reefs. My sire and mother are not known."

She pulled a long quartz crystal from her garment, glanced into it and gasped.

"What," he said. Tension knotted his muscles. He'd stupidly left his crystal at Becca's parents' time share in their haste to get to the restaurant.

She held the crystal to his face.

The mantle of the earth was shifting, creating what land forms called a quake along the bottom of the sea. This could cause a tidal wave to reach the land. They had to leave immediately to ensure they could travel safely through the portal before it was damaged.

Would Becca leave her parents so soon? She could stay on land with Gareth until he could return to her. It could not be until the solstice in what the humans in the northern hemisphere on earth called winter. And that was if the portal was not damaged.

Becca and Mike laughed about someone named Cheryl and deadlines.

Cerissa stared into the crystal. "The portal is safe, for now."

Ethan put his hand on Becca's nape. "Becca."

She spun to face him, laughing.

"An earthquake rumbles through the depths," he said.

The color drained from her face. "What happens now?"

Cerissa continued to stare into the quartz. Mike put his arm around her. "The portal remains undamaged. But the plate shift is not stopping."

"Gareth." Becca ran to her parents. Ethan stained to hear her spoken words or catch her thoughts. He discerned, "danger," and "he must leave, he is not safe."

He? Not we? His chest tightened. Becca hurried toward him. Janet carried Gareth and Rob put money on the table.

Becca squeezed Cerissa's shoulder. "Thanks, Cerissa." She hugged Mike. "Bye."

They walked to the vehicle and settled Gareth inside. Becca sat in the front seat with her father driving, directing him to Waimea Canyon, wiping tears off her cheeks.

"Do you have to leave now?" Janet said. She was weeping.

Becca wanted to be with her parents. How could he wrench her away from them?

"No," he said. "Becca and Gareth may stay on land. Only I must go."

Janet stroked Gareth's face. "It's not fair," she said.

Rob stopped the vehicle. Becca wrenched the door open, unfastened Gareth, and took him in her arms.

"No," Janet screamed.

Rob rushed to her side.

"Mom." Becca stepped toward her mother.

"I've got your pills," Rob said.

"I don't want my pills, I want my daughter and grandson," Janet screamed.

Gareth whimpered.

Ethan couldn't bear it. How could Becca be with him in the Garnet City, knowing she'd caused her mother to be ill again? Her beautiful spirit would wither with guilt. He turned away from her and made his way toward the portal.

How could he still walk and breathe? His heart and soul were dissolving.

"Ethan?" Becca screamed. She ran to him, stumbling on the rough terrain. He caught her in his arms and the claws around his heart loosened.

"Mom. Ethan's crystal. We left it on the cushions where I was feeding Gareth. Look through it. We'll see each other."

Janet's sobs subsided. Becca grasped his arm as if she would never let him go. "I love you Mom and Dad," she said. "I will be with Ethan. Take us home, darling."

Starved for the taste of her, he claimed her mouth in a too-brief kiss then led them to the portal.

She caressed his jaw. "Take us home, please."

He pulled them inside and kissed her as Gareth squirmed in her arms. The journey was short and the red hills of the Garnet City loomed in the distance as they walked out.

ⳋⳃⳋⳃ

Becca's anger simmered as she remembered Ethan moving quickly to the portal—without them. He was going to leave her and Gareth on land in his misguided attempt to spare her the pain of leaving her parents.

Lara and Thorion came forward along the path, chanting words of thanks for their safe return.

"He is nourished?" Thorion looked at Gareth.

She nodded and Thorion reached to take Gareth in his arms.

"We have missed him, and you," Lara said.

Gareth squeezed Lara's finger.

"The quake?" Ethan said.

"Should not bring damage to the Garnet City," Thorion said.

Lara looked toward the portal and shuddered. "Is good you are home."

"Could you take Gareth for a bit?" Becca said. She struggled to keep her voice calm.

Lara looked at Becca in question. She seemed satisfied with Becca's unspoken answer and said "Of course."

She and Thorion sang to Gareth in perfect harmony as they walked along the channel to the entrance of the city.

When she could no longer hear their voices, she rounded on Ethan, shaking with anger. "You would have left us."

He moved closer but she stepped back. "Becca."

"You had no right to make that decision for me, that I would stay without you."

Squawk.

Nudge lifted her head out of the channel, then jumped high, drenching Ethan.

He muttered a curse and sat quickly to yank off his shorts before he took he took sea form. He pulled off his shirt then clamped his hand around her ankle as he slipped into the channel, bringing her with him. Her tail unfurled and he pulled her dress over her head in a sodden heap on the path. The youth that kept the path free of debris would collect it later. He took hold of her waist and fused his mouth to hers.

Despite her anger, she kissed him back. She would always kiss him back.

He tore his mouth from hers and tugged on her nipples the way he knew she loved.

"Stop distracting me," she said.

He tugged on her necklace. "You like my distracting."

He was going to leave her. She had to remember that. She pulled his hair, hard. "How could you leave us?"

She submerged and grabbed hold of Nudge's fins. The dolphin propelled her through the channel to their chamber and left her. She pulled herself from the water and waited to take land form.

A feast awaited them. Shells were piled with lobster, shrimp, and mackerel as well as sea vegetables she was still learning the names for and a goblet of the peach flavored amber liquid she loved so much. She looked at her tail. She loved the shades of crimson and blue but wondered why it was taking so long to take land form.

Ethan surfaced and pulled himself out of the water, tangling his tail with hers. She clutched his shoulders. "Something is wrong. My land form—"

He cupped her cheek and pinched her waist. She felt the familiar tingling, then her legs, tangled with his. His erection pressed against her.

"I did not wish it."

She pushed away from him. "You did not wish it? You control this?"

She turned away from him, couldn't look at him.

He was right behind her, his breath against her cheek. "Only until you will you learn your fins, I may control this. I was afraid you will flee before you understand."

She whirled to face him. His turquoise eyes held such tenderness she went weak in her knees and had to focus on what she had to say. "I hate that you control this or thought you knew what was best. I thought everything was based on my free will." She drank in his broad, toned shoulders, smooth, golden chest and erection, barely contained in his loincloth.

Would he always look like this? How would she win any fight, ever?

His mouth quirked into a smile. "I do not wish a fight with you, Becca. And we will not age as land forms. Lara and Thorion exist for three hundred earth revolutions."

Damn.

He read her thoughts.

He slid his finger along her cheek. "I...what you say?...screwed up. You weep for leaving your parents. Your grief dissolves me inside. I must ease or stop pain for you always. But I would not be whole without you."

She swallowed hard. She wanted to plaster her mouth on his and lose herself in his touch, but this was too important. "Ethan, we must discuss things and make decisions together."

He nodded and nuzzled her neck. She wrapped her arms around his lean, hard waist. Her stomach growled.

He carried her to the bed then arranged morsels from the buffet on a large, flat shell and set it on a table next to the bed. He filled a glass with amber liquid and handed it to her. She drank it all. He took the glass and poured her more, then took some for himself.

She watched his throat as he swallowed the liquid. How could that arouse her?

He came to her, settled her between his legs, and took the empty glass from her hand. "You wish more?"

"Not to drink," she said, a huskiness to her voice.

He pressed a bite of shrimp to her lips. She chewed. He nuzzled her neck and caressed her breasts. A drop of milk dribbled out and he licked it.

She twisted away from him. "Gareth, he must be hungry."

He pulled her back against him and held a bite of lobster dripping in her favorite savory sauce to her lips. "He is sated and will sleep after the journey. He is greedy for you, as I am."

She devoured it then sucked the sauce from his fingers. She felt him grow harder against her. He fed her until she waved him away and turned her face into his neck, inhaling his scent of cool water.

He tightened his arms around her. "I will leave you for eco missions, perhaps when the quake stops."

Lara had explained to her that sea forms considered themselves stewards of the depths and watched over all life forms but faced peril in the depths when they did so.

She trailed kisses down the hard column of his throat. "I know this," she said.

"You may not come with me until you learn your fins, and there is Gareth," he said.

She took his face in her hands. "I'm a cop's kid. We never knew for sure if he would be safe when he left for work. But he told us we meant everything to him, so he'd be damned if some thug got him. He worked undercover for a while, pretending to be what he is not, someone bad. He had to stop, that's when Mom had her first bad spell."

He traced her lips with his thumb. "Enforcing laws on land has danger. I feel as your sire and will take care so I return to you."

She smiled into his eyes. "We kiss now. After couples fight, they kiss and make up." She stroked his erection that strained against his loincloth. "Then there's makeup sex—joining," she said.

He scowled. "I do not wish to fight with you."

She pulled his erection free. "From what I've heard, make up sex is hot."

He looked puzzled.

She pushed him on his back and straddled him. "Hot means very, very good," she said.

He took hold of her waist, lifted her; eased her onto his cock, sliding along every nerve ending until he hit her G-spot. He pressed his thumb over her bundle of nerves, bringing her to instant climax.

She screamed his name. His eyes never left her face. "Our joining is always very, very good, Becca."

Was he pissed?

Still inside her, he rolled them so she was on her back with her legs wrapped around his waist.

"It is, darling, always," she said, gasping as he pumped into her the way she loved.

He smiled. "I like hot make up sex. But no anger, first. Nothing bad between us, Becca, ever." He punctuated every word with a thrust.

"We'll figure out," she moaned. "I promise."

And they did.

THE END

About the Author

Tara Eldana, pen name, is an award-winning staff writer for a weekly community newspaper chain in metro Detroit. She became hooked on romance fiction when her eleventh grade English teacher rejected the book report she wrote, saying the book was much too easy for her, and insisted she read and report on Daphne du Maurier's *Rebecca*. She had read Margaret Mitchell's *Gone With the Wind* that previous summer.

Eldana took a long road through J-school, graduating from Oakland University in Rochester, Michigan in '95, just shy of 20 years after she finished high school, raising a couple kids, working part-time, and doing her homework while her husband and kids watched TV. Still she found time to read what her kids called her "mush books."

She loves the romance genre and loves letting her characters take control of their stories. Eldana is a member of the Greater Detroit Romance Writers of America. Contact her at taraeldana.com, Facebook or Twitter.